TWELFTH MAN

HOWARD HOCKIN

In one split-second, one singular moment in time, I am detached from the real world. This cannot be real, surely? This did not happen. How could it? I was at rock bottom, lower than I have ever been before, to a place closer to hell than five relegations could ever take me. All around me, there is something happening that I know instantly is never to be repeated, never matched, never beaten. In basic terms, pure, unadulterated carnage. Bedlam – there's another word, and joy like I have never experienced before, and perhaps never will again. I am hugging three friends at the same time. I am hugging strangers. I am moving in random directions, I am in the row behind, I am in the aisle. I am bouncing off seats, and it hurts, and I could not care less. The hurt is over. A guttural sound that is unique to this moment in time resonates around the entire ground. I notice the faces of those beside me, wide-eyed, pure happiness, the faces of those who, and this is no exaggeration, have seen their lives transformed with one swing of a boot. Wild screams, arms raised to the heavens, uncontrollable, unrehearsed, unbelievable. None of us know how to act so we revert to primitive beings. A friend appears from nowhere, one who was sat ten rows away and he jumps on my back. I don't know where I am anymore. Songs spring into life, but it is mostly still screaming. I take my first glance towards the pitch since I last looked to check the linesman did not have his flag raised. The scenes on the pitch are similar to those in the stands. I will relive this moment a thousand times, but it cannot match what I feel right now. Bottle it up, and drink it in. I wish I could. I've fallen in love all over again.

This - THIS - is how it can feel to be a football fan.

My name is Colin Michael Sweeney, and I am a football supporter. I would say I am quite a passionate one, if I was sure what that entailed, which I am not. All I can say is that I have loved football since I was five years old, I think about it a lot, too much, and if you're reading this you are either related to me, or feel the same.

I was named after Colin Bell, one of Manchester City's greatest ever players, and Mike Summerbee, his legendary teammate when Manchester City won the league in 1968. My mum never knew this, as my dad was well aware she would not agree to such reasoning. Instead, he simply persuaded her over time that Colin and Michael were two great names for a baby born in 1976. If I had been a girl, there would have been some awkward conversations. Michaela, perhaps? Dad says Colin was the King, the greatest of all time, and always will be.

I have a story to tell. I don't know what that story is yet, but as a football fan I know there will be one. There always is. So this will be mine. Of a single football season, and what that entails. The highs, the lows, the stress, the joy, the pain, the emotion, the journey. The bar snacks. Where will it take me? We will see.

As you have surely already worked out, my team is Manchester City. It is the summer of 2011, and they will start the approaching season as possible title contenders, and while they have not won the Premier League before, with their new wealth, expectations have changed. Their cross-town rivals, and the reigning champions, Manchester United, will be clear favourites, with Chelsea 2nd favourites. City are 4/1. Even those odds seem impossible to comprehend for a fanbase used to mediocrity and false hope. A one-in-five chance sounds good to me.

But enough about Manchester City, for now. This book follows a season in their history, but it's not really about them. It's about being a fan, and the life we all lead, week in, week out. It's a full-time job, when you place your emotions in the hands of other people, and organise your week around a fixture list, and this I hope will paint a vivid picture of it all.

In The Beginning

I have been in love with football since the early 1980s, since the moment I understood what it was I was watching. I don't know why I fell in love with the game, and even now I find it hard to put into words why football enthrals me more than anything else. After all, I will watch pretty much any sport, apart from dressage or ice skating, but football reigns supreme, well ahead of my next favourite sport, cricket. I guess I don't need to determine why it is much more important than anything else. It just is. Billions feel the same. Twenty-two players kicking a ball around a pitch is what we want to spend much of our spare time watching. Add to that the culture which accompanies the sport, the simplicity of it in its basic form that allows anyone to play it anywhere there is a bit of space and some jumpers for goalposts, and perhaps it is less of a mystery. Perhaps football offers more drama than any other sport, but I am not totally convinced. If like me you can fall in love with football in the UK in the 1980s, a period of hooliganism, tragedy, crumbling stadiums and a government who hated fans, then you were set for life.

Whatever the reasons, I was hooked. City were my team, as maybe even at that early age they fitted my personality best, irrespective of my dad supporting them. He did not push me to follow his path, but I wanted to. He used to take me to other grounds too until I found my calling. Gigg Lane to see Bury, even Old Trafford when City were not playing. But there could only be one team. City fit me like a glove. Lacking in arrogance, as they did not have the success to back it up, they were far from the worst team in the world either, and considered a big team, of sorts, with a rich history. There was always the feeling that better times lay ahead, but they rarely arrived, until I was well into adulthood. All fans feel that though, perhaps out of hope more than expectation. One of my first memories was standing in the kitchen listening to City get relegated on the radio in 1983. It set the scene nicely for the years that followed. Nevertheless, when you are obsessed with football, you do not fall out of love with it should your team fail, and you choose your team for life. It may be the longest relationship you have. For some, the team you support is not optional, but passed down from generation to generation, like a bloodline. You support the same team as your dad, who supports the same team as his dad. Blue's the nicest colour, so it was pretty easy to follow the crowd.

Where precisely did it all begin? I've no idea. I don't believe those that seem to have a crystal-clear recollection of their first ever game as a child. For many years I meant to ask my dad which game it was, but it's too late now. It's not that important, but it would be nice to look it up. The result was probably irrelevant in developing my love for the game. It's the occasion and the spectacle, the views, the noise and the smells (good and bad) that seal the deal. There's no other place like it. I imagine it may have been during the 1977/78 season, as I know he once took me before I could walk properly (mum once said I learned very quickly, though). One evening, I sit at home, and read match reports from that campaign, and imagine what it must have been like to be there, with my dad, for the first time.

A Life More Ordinary

I should probably tell you a little about myself, though very briefly, as there is little to tell. I feel I am sometimes defined by the football team I support, rather than by my other characteristics. I think I am loyal and kind and I am shy and I lack drive, and I don't like drawing attention to myself. I like sitting down, and suffer from insomnia as I can never turn my brain off. Maybe I would be a rich man if I wrote down my middle-of-the-night thoughts, but I never do. Maybe if I had pursued my business ideas, such as producing tuna in 30% bigger tins, and takeaways that offer different sized portions, I wouldn't be sat here, in the near dark, typing my thoughts. Maybe.

I work in insurance, at a low level, and I despise every minute of it. My boss hates me, that much is clear. He lives in a big house in Bowden and it is common knowledge that he cheats on his wife on a regular basis. No one seems that bothered, least of all his wife. I like my colleagues, most of them, and flexi time means I can finish early when football fixtures overlap with work, but otherwise there is little to recommend about my life right now. I am in a rut, and do not know how to do anything about it. The pay is poor, and the job menial. Like everyone else who has not completed their life goals, I feel I deserve better. But better is not just going to fall into my lap.

Football is going to be my emotional crutch over the coming year more than ever, and there's an additional reason for that - I have recently split up from a fairly long-term relationship. I was with Claire for seven years, and it is hard to deal with that in my head. To deal with such a seismic change. To have no one to tell me I am wrong, stupid, clever, too drunk, or that I have my jumper on back to front.

Being single has changed the dynamics of being a football fan. Before, I lived a life of compromise. If I wanted a day out with the football crowd, then I was obliged to give something back. A night out with Claire's friends, some of whom I liked, and others who don't possess a single redeeming feature. Claire wouldn't have seen this as a trade-off, but I did. You never knew when something would be arranged for you. You thought you could watch City in the pub, with a pass for at least four hours, but then you discovered Claire had accidentally booked us in to go to Steve and Ellie's for a dinner party. She knew City were playing, she knew. It was a test.

Our biggest argument, that resulted in us blanking each other for two days and me sleeping on the couch, revolved around football. Claire finds – sorry, found - my emotional attachment to some rich men kicking a ball impossible to fathom, in the same way I struggle to understand her love of reality TV. I was once so down after a bad result, that she demanded I give up my season ticket, as it was affecting the relationship. I didn't know how to demonstrate to her that I can never let go, and that my football team means everything to me, but then I can't put it into words why this is. At least our couch was comfy. The fog lifted as I got over the result, as every fan always does, and we returned to our normal life. Claire grew to love summers and international breaks as she knew my mood was less prone to fluctuation.

Now, none of my past responsibilities with Claire matter. I can commit myself to my one true love, football. I can go where I want, when I want. The world is my oyster, and it's nice not to have commitments. But a part of me misses the old life. Coming home to an empty house after a nice win is not quite the same. Being able to do whatever I want is not the utopia I had imagined. It's not good for my liver either.

State Of Play

As for my team, there is plenty of optimism in the air. The squad is a good mix of, well, everything. Just three years after an investment group from the United Arab Emirates with too much money to comprehend took over, it has it all. Players that have come through the academy, such as Micah Richards, a powerhouse at right-back. A couple of pre-takeover gems that have matured into key cogs in the machine, Pablo Zabaleta and Vincent Kompany. With Financial Fair Play regulations on the horizon, City spent wildly and aggressively after the takeover to get themselves a squad worthy of competing at the top before the drawbridge came down. You can see some of the results of the scattergun approach, with the likes of Wayne Bridge on the payroll, and Emmanuel Adebayor once more loaned out, this time to Tottenham Hotspur. There's Argentinean class upfront with Sergio Aguero and Carlos Tevez, though the latter has already threatened to leave, and like his previous clubs it feels like he is merely passing through. Complimenting them is the big lad up front, Edin Dzeko. Good feet for a tall man. There's the steel of Nigel De Jong and the wisdom and steady hand of Gareth Barry. There's the varied beauty of Yaya Toure and David Silva, who along with Sergio Aguero I still struggle to comprehend play for my club. Silva is a magician, a bundle of joy, of perfect ball control, body feints, delicious passes, a player that purrs and makes you happy to pay to watch the game. A metronome around whom many attacking phases focus. If they stay for just a few years, I will still feel very lucky.

There's the safe hands of Joe Hart, another youth product of sorts, the rock-hard Aleksandar Kolarov, the experience of Gael Clichy, the enigmas that are Samir Nasri and Mario Balotelli.
It may well be the most cosmopolitan squad the club has ever seen. England, Argentina, Ivory Coast, Spain, France, The Netherlands, Italy, Bosnia, Serbia, Montenegro, Chile, Belgium

and Romania. It has crept up on me, but when I cast an eye over the squad, its potential dawns on me, and I wonder how far the players can take City.

I read an article about Edin Dzeko, and his tough upbringing, playing football and trying to survive in the shadow of the Bosnian War Of Independence. I cannot comprehend such a life.

I'd rather all players had an idyllic childhood, but fans love these stories, of triumph over adversity. Perhaps they think it makes such players more driven, and thus more likely to succeed. The more adversity overcome, the less likely a player is to throw it all away. So often you see articles about South American players whose tough upbringing made them, learning their craft "on the streets". Their escape route, perhaps.

Summer Break

I am fairly content, despite life's travails and the fall out of a broken relationship. It is summer after all, and the sun is often out, not always a sure-thing in England. The fug of the split hits me occasionally, normally when sleep once more evades me, but I am getting by, and trying to be positive. I resolve to think about other things. My football club won their first trophy in 35 years, the FA Cup, the previous month, and it was emotional. As soon as I heard Abide With Me at Wembley, I was welling up. Stood there, experiencing it live, not on my couch. I spent my childhood watching other teams win the FA Cup, and I dreamed of one day seeing my team there. The FA Cup is special to me, and always will be. The day of the final used to be an occasion for all fans, when tribalism was an alien concept. The TV coverage was all day, in a time when there were only three channels to choose from. You'd see the players eating their breakfast, getting on and off the coach, and this was part of the many hours of broadcast before the match kicked off. The Road To Wembley, that began nine months previous, way down the football pyramid. All culminating in this day. Football tradition, writ large. And it was all fascinating, unlike nowadays, when choice has destroyed my attention span and concentration levels.

What was I talking about? Yes, I saw City for the first time at Wembley in 1999, but that was a play-off final, and play-offs weren't even a thing when I was growing up, so it was not quite how I had imagined my first visit. City scored two goals in injury time and won on penalties, so it was quite the day, all things considered. Rained a lot, not that we cared. The place was showing its age, but it was still a special place. Walking up Wembley Way for the first time is something that stays with you. Spotting the Twin Towers felt like being the first to see Blackpool Tower on a childhood trip to the seaside. And 12 years later, with very wealthy owners propelling City to new heights, I was back, twice, to see City defeat cross-city rivals Manchester United in the semi-final and Stoke City in the final. The club was different now, and my journey was going in a different direction to that of my youth. This was no bad thing.

Many long-term fans may feel uncomfortable about this new path, but much of that is based on misplaced nostalgia. As many of you know all too well, it is not more fun following a poor football team. The triumphs, should they arrive, can be appreciated more than when your team is expected to win everything, not that my team is at that point just yet, and may never be. But nostalgia is overrated. Following my team as it declined on and off the pitch was a horrible experience. It felt like it would never end, and that this was my life forever. Many older blues talk with fondness about the trips to Macclesfield, York, Northampton Town and more, but were they enjoying the experiences at the time? However, for many fans, it gave us our gallows humour and the perseverance that is part of many a club's DNA, but we all wanted better than this life. Much better.

There is one thing that keeps such fans going in such situations, that kept me going for two decades and more. Hope. Because without hope, what is there? And what is the point? Your club owner may have spent the summer selling off the ground, coming off the back of three successive relegations, sold all your star players, installed the worse manager known to humanity, changed the home kit to turquoise with a lime sash, doubled season ticket prices and installed a huge statue of himself outside the ground, but any new season still brings hope.

So every August, you may be happy with the summer transfer business, or you may not. Your club may be favourites for relegation. You may hate the manager. But there's always a chance, always, that things will be OK. Or better than that. Your club may exceed expectations, buck the trend, and be a contender. Every team in every league starts the season with that chance, however small it may be. Fans need that, it's our oxygen. Going to watch your team knowing they will lose is a poisoned chalice. Done out of duty more than anything else. Perhaps because you may have nothing better to do.

We need each other though. I have watched games by myself at home, when ill, skint, or due to other one-off circumstances. I find it unbearable. Watching a game with other fans creates a cultural connection and a sense of belonging. This offers a sense of togetherness and group identity. Perhaps it gives life more meaning too, when you form that bond and support a common cause with others. For all our faults, fans are the lifeblood of the game. Imagine football without fans, and what a soulless pursuit it would be, little more than a TV show. It barely seems worth it. Worth considering, the next time a fanbase has to travel 300 miles for a Friday night game, and the last train home departs at half-time.

Routines

Football fans tend to like a routine. For some, where the day is put aside for the game, there is a set pre-match pub, though this may vary according to kick-off times, and days. There is set match-going attire, that again can change as the seasons do. There are the same people to meet, the same route to the ground, the same concourse spot at half-time. As for the pub, I have reached the age where good beer and serenity is preferred over noise, music and plastic pint pots. And so as a new season arrives, millions of people across the world change their routine, switching to "season mode". There's been ample time to peruse the fixture list, even if every game is subject to change, and plans have been made for the nine months ahead.

Texts are exchanged amongst this season's match-goers and pre-match pub regulars about plans for the following season, with a fortnight to go. Impatience has kicked in, so we may as well have a run-up at this. Are we happy to stick with the same pub? Should we wait and see what the weather is like, in case a bigger beer garden is preferable for a sunny day? Anyone got a spare ticket for the Swansea match? It's close now, and the anticipation is back, a new season, and who knows what it will bring? Dave is after a spare, an early heads-up, as he wants to bring his brother. We say we'll look out for one. Colin is his best bet, he's always exchanging tickets, hanging around outside the ground pre-match waiting to meet up with someone.

I have plenty of hope for the new season. City's away kit is on-brand, a thing of beauty, red and black stripes, harking back to one of our greatest ever kits, worn in the 1969 FA Cup final. City have signed Sergio Aguero from Atlético Madrid, a transfer that excites me more than any other in living memory. For the first time, I think my club has signed someone who I know to be world-class. Also in is Samir Nasri, the mercurial Frenchman, and with a lot of unwanted players out the door, this team looks pretty exciting. One of the many great things about following a side on the up, is the excitement of possible incoming transfers, without the worry of transfer outgoings, losing the perpetual fear of your best players being picked off by bigger, more successful clubs. This is a long journey though. Winning the league is a much bigger task than winning a cup, so perhaps patience is required. What that cup victory did was open the door to further success. It feels that after decades the monkey is off the club's back. So the hope is there, and so is the expectation. A chance to look down league tables, and not up.

Odd Years

Then there is that impatience once more. Summer can drag without football, and a year that ends in an odd number brings with it almost three months without meaningful action. I always like a break from games, because the stress of following a team can be overwhelming when you take such things too seriously, as many of us do. But soon, that break becomes monotonous, and you want to get back on the horse. To go through the rollercoaster of emotions once more, spread out over a nine-month period. Someone once asked me how I cope with the stress of being a football fan. The simple and truthful answer is that I don't. But I still need football, more than ever. I hate it, I love it, I need it.

I help fill the time with a week in Greece with friends, enjoying sandy beaches, turquoise seas, blue skies and endless good food and drink. I don't want to come back, but holidays are a brief detachment from reality, and I exit Manchester Airport to a wall of drizzle hanging in the cool night air. It is colder than I thought possible for July. I pay far too much for a taxi, and drag my suitcase into my flat, exhausted, yet well aware I won't be able to get to sleep for hours. I look in a mirror and my heart drops with the realisation that my tan has already faded. Back to reality.

But would I really want to stay in Greece? I could think of worse places to be, but soon I would miss the place I call home. And I'd miss that matchday routine. My friends, the ground, even the tram home.

But for now, it's a waiting game. The rest of a football-free summer is filled with tiny joys, like the fixture list, that allows you to visualise the season ahead. You play everyone twice so it hardly holds any surprises, but it is always of interest to see what the first game is, when the two Derby Days fall, the Christmas schedule and the run-in. The Boxing Day fixture is a big one, praying for a home fixture, to escape after Christmas has come and gone.

Then there is the transfer gossip, which has been ruined by the internet. Too many links, too many lies, it is hard to know the truth anymore. Better to celebrate a signing when they are pictured holding up the shirt. Until then, rumours are just that. Let's not pretend we don't get a buzz from them though – especially when your team has a "war chest" to spend.

The Price Of Progress

There is always a football story to mull over, even over the summer. The latest example is a predictable media outcry over City announcing naming rights for their nine-year-old stadium. City left Maine Road in 2003, and it hurt, but I understood it. This was the price of progress. Most teams will move to a new home at some point. You leave behind a treasure trove of memories, but the opportunity to form new ones remains, wherever you may be. Maine Road was opened in 1923, the same year as Wembley, and was full of character. But it was a mess, and being slap bang in the middle of an inner-city area, it could not be redeveloped or expanded to an acceptable level. The move has proved to be the right decision. Anyway, this new stadium has no real name, and little heritage, so selling the rights to the name is not a problem for me. Perhaps of greater interest is the size of the deal, valued at £400m over a ten-year period, that has reignited insinuations that City fiddle the books. If it buys some great players, I couldn't care less. Call it what you want, when I get in a taxi before a match, the conversation will remain the same: "to the ground, please".

I received my football education at Maine Road, but the brutal truth is that I do not miss the place much. I have moved on, in the same way that one day that hearing the name Claire will not result in a period of melancholy.

The stadium was not demolished until 2004, a year after City left. There was even talk of it being maintained, Stockport County mentioned as an option. But that never transpired. Soon it was a "sea of rubble at the end of the street". And as fans we think about the effect leaving a stadium on us, and the memories it provided. But the bigger effect is on the community, which often relies on the match-day crowd to not only prosper, but survive.

In Moss Side, the pubs will dwindle away now, much of their business gone. The shops may struggle too. The housing estate, Maine Place, was built eventually, a small plaque where the centre circle once stood the only evidence of what once existed there. Gone from our sight, but not from our memory, eight years ago the Wembley Of The North was no more.

Football Grounds

Night games were always the best. But they were better at Maine Road not because it was a better ground than its successor, but because it was hidden. Hidden in the middle of a maze of terraced houses and dark, dank alleyways. You could sense the ground, because there was a huge light source casting shade somewhere in the distance, like a UFO rooted on a forest floor. Then you'd turn a corner, and there it was. The ground as you always saw it, according to the direction you approached it from. Maybe the Kippax looming large behind the brick turnstiles. Or the main stand and entrance in front of the forecourt.

Are the grounds themselves a major reason we all fall in love with the sport? Every single one unique, with its own memories seeping out of every pore. Try and collate all your footballing memories. Thoughts will turn to classic matches, memorable days at Wembley, favourite players, the lows of relegation, the key moments down the years. For me though, some key memories did not occur on the pitch. Some memories are not footballing moments at all. They are structures. There was the first time I walked out the concourse and saw Wembley laid out before me in 1999. What a dump, but it was Wembley, it meant something. The misshaped Maine Road stands. The Gene Kelly Stand, a temporary stand in the corner without any cover, and my guilt at chuckling at its inhabitants on a rainy day, decked out in cheap macs. The cantilever roof. The floodlights. Outside toilets. And of course the Kippax. The Lowry-like procession of people shuffling towards our sporting place of worship. And often shuffling away.

Some struggle to let go. It's why a rusting blue seat can be found in many a Manchester back garden. Why I have an oil painting of Maine Road up on the wall. After Maine Road closed its doors for the final time, there was an auction for pieces of the items that remained. Prized memorabilia on offer included the boardroom table which fetched a modest £460, the gates from the players' tunnel (£40, if you're wondering), the front doors to the stadium, the City squad's dressing-room door and the door to the manager's office. That's a lot of doors. And some seats of course.

Maine Road was unique, but every ground is. Especially from the air. After all, who doesn't like a nice aerial shot of a football ground? Who hasn't got a little bit giddy looking out of an airplane window as a stadium drifts by underneath? Often, grounds are described by commentators with religious terminology. And in a way it makes sense, the masses converging on one place to pray and seek contentment. The ground represents a club's and its fans' identity.

Close

Pre-season friendlies follow, which for City means a tour of the US. Over there, fans get to see the players close-up, something we rarely get back in England. This is the natural outcome to the distrust football clubs have of fans, that means players at the top level live much of their lives in a bubble. That distrust is understandable to some extent as times have changed. It means almost too much to too many fans, that ramps up tribalism and anger should players fail to reach expectations. Some fans place their esteem and happiness in the hands of football players and managers. Letting us all have open access to their place of work is not to be recommended.

The final game of the tour ends with penalties against LA Galaxy, which City win. The game is utterly meaningless, a chance for the club to make money, spread their global appeal and allow the squad to gain some match fitness. And yet I still feel my heart beat increase and a slither of anxiety kick in at the thought of a penalty shoot-out. During the tour, Mario Balotelli is causing trouble again, in his own unique way. He tries to backheel the ball into the net when through on goal. He misses, and is hauled off by Roberto Mancini. In a pre-season friendly.

City inhabit a different world nowadays. Perhaps all top-level clubs do. Preseason means getting the airmiles in, for two simple reasons. To make money, and to increase a club's global profile, to snare future fans. A child who decides to support Manchester City will eventually become an adult who supports Manchester City, one who the club hope spends thousands of pounds following their team. And perhaps that adult will have children who will follow a similar path.

It never used to be like this. City used to play local clubs, because it made sense and it helped clubs in lower divisions on meagre budgets. Now they must fend for themselves, and I have to watch

City on my computer as dawn breaks. I decide to look up the games for a past preseason to prove my point, and pick the 2002/3 season at random. Unfortunately for my argument, the summer of 2002 saw City travel to Denmark for a round-robin tournament, and play a friendly in Hamburg. They did however also play Bury, Rochdale and Tranmere, which was a testimonial match for Eric Nixon, so if anything this period signified the transitional period as City moved between playing local and playing abroad. What followed would include City setting up their own slightly glamorous pre-season friendly, the winners of which would lift the prestigious Thomas Cook trophy. The new stadium was opened with a 2-1 win over Barcelona, and in 2007, a young hotshot named David Silva scored the decisive goal for the visiting Valencia team. Whatever happened to him?

Getting On

My sister suggests I take up a hobby. She suggests I start running, like she does. Jill has completed marathons, I get dizzy rising from a chair too quickly. I tell her I will consider it. I try painting, as I was quite good at art as a child, but soon realise I have lost the necessary skills or patience to produce anything recognisable. A hundred pounds down the drain, and the flat stinks of white spirit.

I decide I will learn Spanish, and within a week have given that up too, though I can now ask where the station is. So that only leaves one thing. To start a blog and write a diary about the 2011/12 season. I like stories, and I like writing them, though this story will write itself. Let's hope it is worth my time.

So as you can see, that is what I did. And, as I write this having returned from the future, I stuck with it. A lot of my thoughts are not about football, and I am yet to decide whether you will ever read them. But writing has proved to be cathartic, and therapeutic. It helps me make sense of things, to understand why the world and my life is the way it is. Often it makes me feel even worse, but I shall persevere. I have sent some articles to a City fanzine too, and got a buzz seeing my name in print. I am dipping my toes into the world of podcasting, a world I only know because of Ricky Gervais. I hope that things like this will bring me out of my shell. The flip side is that I am committing to my football team in new ways. I will be spending more of each day discussing their progress and am at the mercy of their success or failure. It feels like I cannot walk away now, not even for a few days. My mood will be linked even more intrinsically to my football team than before. It's a dangerous game.

Almost There

Not long to go now. The start of a new season brings with it the delusion that this season, definitely, absolutely, without doubt, I will take my Fantasy Football obligations seriously. I pore over the options, losing almost an afternoon devising the perfect team. This is the one. The season that I prove how much I know about football. I can have three City players in my squad, so I plump for Joe Hart, David Silva and Sergio Aguero.

As for United players? I am not allowed, should I wish to remain in one of the private leagues set up for City fans. But if I want to succeed at Fantasy Football, I can't ignore the squad of the reigning champions, due to such pettiness. I burn my bridges and pick Rio Ferdinand and Wayne Rooney. And as always, I look at my final squad and fail to understand how anyone else could beat it.

Sleepless Nights

So, about that insomnia I briefly mentioned previously. It comes and it goes, without warning. I struggle to turn my brain off when it is time for sleep. Too many thoughts continue to race round my head, too many anxieties. I've tried everything, to no avail. The only thing that partially works is listening to my own voice on a podcast.

I lie in bed one night, sleep evading me, thinking about being back in my usual seat at The Etihad. I can't wait. New name, same seat. My decision about where to sit in the ground is a simple one. I sit in the cheap seats. It may be out of necessity, but If I ever win the lottery, I reckon I would remain where I am. That is where my friends are, and that is where most of the life is, in a world of sanitised fully-seated Premier League stadia. Corporate areas are creeping round the ground surely but slowly, as income streams become more and more important, as the atmosphere is sucked out of many top flight grounds. You can already be reprimanded for standing up. But a modern stadium means you can see the pitch wherever you are, so I am not too bothered where I sit. Every angle comes with its advantages and disadvantages. As long as I am not alone, I am happy.

Pub Talk

"If all the seats in the ground were the same price, where would you sit?"

"I'd stay where I am."

"Really? In the corner of the 2nd tier?"

"Yeah, why not. Am used to it, it's near the away fans, get a good view of the action at this end, and I know everyone around me."

"Well OK, let's pretend that it's a new ground, all your friends will sit exactly where you choose, and not moan about it. Where do you pick then?

"Hmm. Well, directly behind a goal I reckon, or a corner is fine also. Let's be honest, the half-way line means you can see everything well enough, but are not close to anything either. And the quietest people would still migrate there."

"When did we last belt out a song?"

"That's not the point. I still like the idea of being in a noisy section, even if I'm not key to that. Anyway, giving it some more thought, City always kick the same way in the 2nd half, and I've no idea why. So I would look to be behind that goal. Best view of any late victories. Not super low, as low seats are the worse, you can't see the opposite end of the pitch at all. Not too high either, as I'd feel isolated. So perhaps about half-way up."

"Yep, fair enough. Now City are quite good now though, I'd plump for the opposite end, near where we are now, for the enjoyment factor of the away fans. Plenty of noise there too."

"I see that. I would never want to be right next to them, but within singing distance makes sense. Just not the half-way line, and not in the gods. I still want to feel a part of it all, for now."

I'm having this discussion with Stuart, who has been going to see City since 1962, to be precise. Stuart is the go-to guy when you need information on City, every bit as good as Google. Tremendous knowledge. If you need to know what the score was between City and Bolton Wanderers in November 1995 (1-0 win, Nicky Summerbee), then he will almost certainly know. I admit to feeling pretty smug on the rare occasion he can't remember something, which I subtly look up on my phone, then pretend to have a Eureka! moment approximately ten minutes later.

The Mask Of Truth

It's time to admit it. No one may ever read these words anyway, so I may be speaking to myself. But sometimes admitting things to yourself is the first step towards making things better. Fact is, my perceived happiness is a mask. I am not happy, and I am relying on my football team changing that. I am not happy because I feel more alone than ever.

My dad is not well. I could see the deterioration in his health approach from a distance. It was the small things at first. Forgetfulness here and there. His ability to name any City players across three decades, and have a story about them, waned. Sentences that tailed off. My phone call from him, set to 7pm every Tuesday and Thursday after he had finished his tea, became more irregular. Occasionally he would phone twice on the same night. When he forgot where he had parked his car, the writing was on the wall. Alzheimer's disease, which means some days he can appear normal and alert, some days less so. And by now, the normal days are few and far between.

Now he is in a care home, and I feel guilt for abandoning him. There was no other option, but this is no way for a full life to end. I can think of nothing crueller than the mind going before the body, nothing. I can't care for him, I have to work to survive, and my two sisters live away. They had ambition, and it took them to London and Auckland.

As for dad, maybe I will write soon about our life together watching City. But I don't feel up to it right now. All I know is I just want the season to start. I feel adrift, and I need something to focus on, something to make me smile.

Football Without Fans

The Community Shield is pointless to me, a glorified friendly and nothing more, a game I have never attended, as I have better things to spend my meagre wages on. Clubs and managers love to count it as a trophy, as it makes them look more successful. Each to their own, and this game still manages to drag me down after City contrive to throw away a two-goal lead to lose 3-2 to hated rivals Manchester United.

Hated rivals, What a silly term. Do I hate them? I guess so, though I am not sure what I am hating here. Their essence, their entire existence, the players, manager and every individual fan? It's nonsense really. You can hate a version of people though. My oldest friend is a United fan, an erudite, sensible, educated man. Change the subject to football though, and he regresses to a caveman – in my opinion.

Already there is another tinge of annoyance. City play their opening game of the season against Brendan Rodger's Swansea City on a Monday night, after 18 other teams' campaigns have begun. Monday night games are an abomination, especially for the first game of the season. But this is football now. Money talks, for City, from TV companies, from anyone. Games can be played at any time, on any day, or so it feels at times. Football without fans is nothing, we are always told. But for how long? The fans are needed, but not necessarily in the ground. Clubs pretend to be a community hub, which in many respects they clearly are, but they do little to stand up for fans welfare, as it would result in losing money.

We are so compliant. We have continued to fill stadiums as prices have rocketed by almost 1000% since the start of the Premier League in 1992. We prefer to fight rival fan bases rather than fight for our own rights. Tribalism has hindered the common cause.

I'm cranky. Work is dragging me down. I'll try not to moan as much in future, I promise. Whether I succeed depends on my football team.

Reboot

The first home game of a season is something special. Time to catch up, and start afresh. If you're lucky no coat will be required, and summer will still be in full swing. Though for a night match, all this becomes redundant. Maybe that is the real reason I am annoyed. Little chance to show off my tan line by taking my watch off. But still, every season is a new chapter, a chance to create new memories. Many of my friends are only seen around football matches, so it's good to get reacquainted, and begin the season with everyone present. We've all survived another year.

Being part of a football family is a perfect indicator of how we can juggle multiple layers of friendship. There is your inner circle, your best friends, with whom you do virtually everything football-related, and a lot more away from the sport. Then there are your good friends, that you may not see as often, but who you could easily holiday with, and care for deeply. Then there is the outer circle. You could have a pint or ten with them at any time, and are totally comfortable in their company, but you could also go many months without seeing or speaking to them, Facebook updates your only clue to the lives they lead. There's even a final layer, those on the periphery. Friends of friends of friends. You could still have a pint or two with them, talk football and more, but you both know deep down that your paths have crossed solely due to others.

There will always be something not quite the same as it was, when you walk into the pub for the first time in August. On this occasion, Mike has turned up at the pub with different coloured hair to last season. Once he was grey, and now he is jet black.

This could be interpreted as some sort of mid-life crisis, but it is more likely that the Just For Men has been dug out because Mike is in a new relationship, his first since a messy divorce three years ago. We rib him mercilessly, as is necessary, but in a gentle way without malice. He is our own Benjamin Button. He wouldn't expect anything less. We ask how it's going with Mary, and then we move on. There's a fair chance we won't ask how she is doing ever again.

That sounds inhumane and cold. Perhaps it is. We merely scratch the surface of our lives in the pub. We talk about little of depth as a group, in fact we don't even talk that much about football. This is our down time, when life's problems are shelved, temporarily. If we talk about something serious, it is more likely to be about someone not present. When serious things happen, and they will, it is unlikely to be debated pre-match. But there is an implicit understanding between all of us – we are there for each other, should anyone need support. It does not need to be said, and if it does, it will be said elsewhere, away from football.

Seeing Mike reminds me of what life can give. He has had his struggles in his past with mental health, and as a result, physical health. There were times when I wondered if I would ever see him again. Expecting the type of call no one wants to take. But here he is, all manicured up, and most importantly, happy. And if he is happy, then I will try to be too, because who knows what lies around the corner?

We laugh and we drink and we talk nonsense. There is no in-depth analysis of what lies ahead. It staggers me sometimes how little I talk football with the people I go to matches with. We lose ten minutes in a remarkably pointless argument, as I try to convince a friend that if eight people play a game of pure chance twice, the odds on the same person winning both games is one in eight, not one in sixty-four. There is advice handed out on the best way to deal with alcohol-induced heartburn, and whether one pint of 8% beer gets you equally inebriated as two pints of 4% beer. And yet online I will lose hours debating City's players, if it's possible to have too many strikers or how Gareth Barry is the most underrated player in the Premier League, every single week.

Another Season Begins

For football fans, there is only one season each year. The first game is a joy, even if it was played at the wrong time. City's debutant Sergio Aguero comes on as a substitute and dazzles, and he is immediately everything I had hoped for. He epitomises the joy of a new signing for a football fan. When they come from foreign shores, it feels more exotic. There is more of the unknown, and it's great to watch a footballer strut his stuff for your team when you have seen precious little of him previously. You learn all about him with every match, and unless it's a disaster, that's a wonderful thing to experience. I knew Aguero was good, very good, but when he fires in from 30 yards on his debut, I am instantly in love. With that cheeky smile, how could I not be? The internet has made discovering a new talent in this way harder, but it is still possible.

It's nice to sit in my seat for the first time each season. It's a security blanket, of sorts. When I visited Maine Road for the final time, I took a small screwdriver in with me. Not to cause violence you understand, but to chisel off my seat number as a small memento. It still sits in my "man drawer" at home, collecting dust (and rust). My club's football ground is like a 2nd home, and when you move, it can be hard to let go.

The usual crowd are all there. Almost. August is holiday season, so there are a couple of seats filled with unfamiliar faces. The section consists mostly of season ticket holders, so you tend to know those around, on top of the fifteen or so friends that sit in the general vicinity. That final level of friends, for whom this is the only place I see many of them. A hello, a chat, a hug for a big goal, and that is it.

Still, it's good to see them. Football brings people together. You form connections with those with a similar passion, that you would otherwise never have met. Frank in front of me, who comes to matches with his daughter, and occasionally his son. He is the silent one, who rarely says anything of note, watching the game passively but intently. His daughter, in her late teens, is passionate about the football, but just as passionate about the many text messages that always arrive on her phone during a match. Three to my left is Simon, a man for whom no performance is good enough. Every player needs shipping out, the jury is out on Roberto Mancini and generally everything sucks. Thankfully, if the prevailing wind is in the right direction, I cannot hear most of what he says. Then there's Stewart behind me, the polar opposite. The most cheerful of men, he sees the promise in the worst of matches. His eternal optimism may not strike a chord with me, but he does make me feel better at times. More importantly, he always has a healthy stash of boiled sweets that he is happy to offer to those around him. To his right is Louise, who has a lovely line in profanities and is the most likely to start up a chant in what is a reserved section of older blues who prefer silence over singing. Chris is the resident coach, the guy that every section of every crowd contains. He is a master tactician, but sadly life has been unkind and his talents have not been recognised, so he sticks to coaching an Under-9 team instead. Every match, he explains regularly where Mancini and the players are going wrong, and how things could be resolved. His talents are wasted in this small corner of a football ground.

The rest of us? Well, I think we're pretty normal. Not the loudest anymore, never were. Not the quietest. Will moan at a misplaced pass but celebrate many goals with real gusto. Middle of the road, where I've always been happy to be.

A Dangerous Path

I'm giving something called Twitter a go. It seems alright, despite all the arguing. I have over 100 followers, mostly football fans, which makes me feel quite important.

It is good for breaking news, whether football or otherwise, and for getting new perspectives on issues I know little about, which is most issues. There seems to be little vetting however, so what is true and what is not? It is addictive, and makes a change from scrolling through baby photos and inspirational messages on Facebook. I can talk to anyone on there too. I wonder if a player will ever reply if I message them?

On The Up

City are entertaining, at levels not seen since Kevin Keegan was in town. Three more wins follow, and there are goals galore. One game stands out, a 1-5 thrashing of Tottenham Hotspur at White Hart Lane. Edin Dzeko scores four goals in the game, quite a rare feat. Later that same day, Manchester United beat Arsenal 8-2, in a day when Manchester rules over North London. I watch all this unfold in a bar on a campsite at Shell Island, on the west coast of Wales. It is a fun weekend, though the wind rattles my tent through both nights, and sleep is fleeting. It is early in the season, but my mind cannot discard the thought that the two Manchester clubs may be fighting for the title during the coming season, and my stomach turns. I do not know how to deal with such pressures. Chelsea might have something to say about that, so perhaps I am getting ahead of myself.

I'm already very, very fond of many of these players. I feel a slither of guilt at the thought of what they could achieve and whether they will replace all my old favourites. This is football on a different level to before, but favourite players are cherished for more than just football prowess alone.

Team News – Manchester City 3 Wigan Athletic 0.

"No Dzeko."

"Eh? Must be injured."

"Nope, he's on the bench."

"What the fuck is Mancini doing? He scored four goals last week."

"Well there must be a good reason for it."

"What possible good reason could there be for benching the player that scored four goals the week before?"

"Dunno, maybe he has a slight knock."

"Wouldn't be on the bench then, would he? Seriously, Mancini is an idiot."

Edin Dzeko is not missed. Sergio Aguero scores a hattrick. I'm in love.

I am going out with friends after the match. For this reason alone, the match takes on even greater importance. I have never been great at dealing with defeat, one of those fans for whom a bad result ruins an entire weekend. It has always been this way, which was inconvenient when my team used to lose more weeks than not. But now that defeats are rarer, they seem to have even greater impact. Because of this, I know I cannot truly switch off and enjoy my night with friends if that night is preceded by a bad City performance. So, they have to win. It's just the way it is, and how it will always be.

Unsung Heroes

As City win 3-2 at Bolton, there is a rare goal for Gareth Barry, City's "Mr Dependable". Barry is one of those players that I imagine every team has. Absolutely crucial to how the team plays, crucial to their success and making the system work, and yet largely ignored and belittled by any other fanbase. A player that is a good litmus test for whether other fans really know their football, or are just pretending. Signed back in 2009 for £12m, Barry is the engine room of the team. He keeps everything ticking over, allowing the more creative players to do their thing. He is as important as any of them. Tidy on the ball, good passer, links defence and midfield, clever, cunning, and a consummate professional. Every team needs a Gareth Barry. It is a role that is often disparaged because what he does well does not make an exciting video reel. He is not a goal scorer, not a blood and thunder defender, not a great header of the ball, not particularly fast, he is just consistently good at performing his role. To call him a water carrier, as Eric Cantona once did about Didier Deschamps, is perhaps accurate even if it was meant as an insult at the time. The modern game is waking up to this, to the importance of their role. They must work hard, and connect defence with midfield. It also helps to be proficient in the dark arts, knowing when to tactically foul, and when to win a foul, something Barry is an expert at. Managers must love players like Barry, as he is never any trouble, something that cannot be said about all the squad at City.

A New Era Dawns

The Champions League group stage is naturally seeded, to remove most of the threat of the biggest teams being knocked out before New Year. It's all to do with coefficients, and City's is poor, so they are in Pot 3 of 4. As always, the draw is strung out to the point where extracting my own teeth with pliers would be preferable, with montages, interviews, and repeated shots of club executives sat with a pen and paper, lest they forget the draw the following day. But the buzz does not wane. This is it. City's first Champions League draw. How exciting. How exotic. A world-famous ex-player is going to read out my team's name, a certain Lothar Matthäus.

Eventually the balls are all picked and unscrewed, and City are in a group with Bayern Munich, Villareal and Napoli. I'm no expert on European football, but that looks tough.

Under The Lights

European nights. The ultimate experience for any football fan, so I am told. What dreams are made of. But not any European night will do. The summit can only be reached via one route, and that is qualifying for the honour to participate in the Champions League. This is it. City have arrived. They are at base camp, ready to ascend. As a youngster, European football seemed very exotic. The names and the kits. The locations seemed to be unobtainable for me, for a child that didn't leave the UK until he was 16, and no one would claim Torremolinos to be exotic. City have qualified for European football in recent years, but that was the Europa League, the more fun version of the Champions League, and qualifying by topping the Fair Play League seemed like a cheat. But when you feed on scraps, you take what you can get.

That reminds me of a phrase that I hate – "typical City". It is ingrained in the DNA of the club – don't get me started on clubs having DNA either – that City will always mess up when there is promise of better times. Maybe they did for a while, but to suggest that City have a monopoly on such behaviour is ridiculous. There are probably fans of many clubs across the country who think their club is no different, and they may have greater reason to think so.

But the phrase pops into my head because of the aforementioned Fair Play League, and how City did their upmost to ruin the last opportunity presented to them. I'm reminiscing again, as I type these words at 1am, wide awake. It was near the end of the 2007/08 season, and Sven-Göran Eriksson was about to get sacked after just one year as City manager. It wasn't official, more an open secret that his time was probably up. City had nothing to play for regarding their league position, but they were on course to qualify for European football if they could just keep out of disciplinary trouble in their final game against Middlesbrough.

So naturally, Richard Dunne got sent off after 15 minutes.

City conceded eight goals too, but who's counting? Somehow, City still qualified for Europe. Then, on a post-season tour of Thailand, City's disgraced owner Thaksin Shinawatra sang "Should I Stay Or Should I Go?" to Sven on a karaoke night, and the next day fired him. And thankfully, soon sold the club, changing everything forever.

Bow Down

Back to the main topic, because sleep is not close, as a car alarm goes off in the distance. I've got an annual review at work tomorrow (today?) and it is playing on my mind. I get nervous in any interview situation; my throat goes dry and I lose my composure. The better I perform, the better my bonus. I keep typing.

It is akin to religious indoctrination to be told that football fans must worship the Champions League. To be told that to conquer that competition is the pinnacle of all footballing achievements. I understand the basic logic, as it allows you to proclaim yourself Champions of Europe, and after that perhaps the world. But are the winning team that? Many times, the team that won the European Cup has failed to win its own domestic league. So, they become Schrodinger's football team. They are both the best team in Europe, whilst not being the best team in their own country.

Nevertheless, it felt like a huge, huge deal for my football club to qualify for the Champions League for the first time. It felt like the club had taken a big leap forward. We're one of the big boys now, the school prefect who gets to tell off pupils for running in the corridor, and has full use of the common room. But now that it has arrived, I realise it's not all that. Not yet, anyway. The common room is just a room, and there's a tear on the pool table.

Maybe I'm just acting like the spurned boyfriend, as City quickly find their inaugural campaign rather tricky.

Yes, Napoli are City's first opponents, and whilst I was not expecting City to terrify Europe, I was not expecting it to be quite so sobering either. City draw 1-1, not the end of the world. But the truth is they were fortunate to avoid defeat. Napoli were bright, energetic and dangerous every time they went forward, making City look lethargic and resembling a rabbit caught in the headlights. Maybe that is a bit harsh, but the game felt like a wake-up call, that any success in this competition may be some time away. The Italian side played in a different way to what I expect on a weekly basis on the league. It felt like a revelation seeing such a clash of styles up close and personal.

I am not too downhearted about the pitfalls of a Champions League campaign. I grew up dreaming of City winning the FA Cup one day, and when my imagination was at its most vivid, perhaps competing for a league title. As a 10-year-old, I didn't dream of the European Cup. It was not part of my world as a supporter. Thus, it is understandable that all I want, for now, is for City to achieve domestic success. I'm not against European glory, obviously, but if I can choose one trophy to win every year until I am no more, then it has to be the Premier League title. The bread-and-butter, 38 games over nine months to determine the best team in the best league in the world. The essence of success for me will always be winning your national league, over any cup competition. But I am also aware that for a global profile, to be considered royalty, European success must follow.

But then that sparks another bone of contention. Two in fact. Club perception and club size. I can deal with both at the same time, by stating that I couldn't care less how my club is perceived, or whether rival fans think the team is great or the club has no history or the club will always be small. Only glory hunters argue such points, as only glory hunters pick a club for such reasons. I didn't pick my football team because they were successful or because I thought they were bigger than every other club. As you know, one of my first memories was getting relegated. No true football fan, using my definition of one, made their choice that way. Arguing over club size is the ultimate willy-waving contest, and a red flag announcing to the world what type of "fan" you are. Yeah, that team across town may have won eight trophies in three years whilst my team has been relegated, but their average attendance has historically been lower than ours, so who is the real winner, eh?

It's the team winning all the trophies, in case you were still undecided. Though football is barely about winning trophies either. You want success, glory and more. But that should never define your support or your club.

These rants are what happens when my brain is deprived of rest.

Anyway, I am just starting a new journey with my football club, and I am getting sleepy. Having grown up wondering if my club would ever win anything, the thought that they may now win the Premier League is EVERYTHING. I am not sure if that will ever change, either. Any progress in the Champions League is merely a bonus, for this season at least. I know I am not alone in this feeling. I feel a sense of contentment to think that City may sell more tickets for FA games compared to Champions League matches. It shows that we respect tradition, and maintain a fondness for domestic football in all its formats. Bucking the trend of kissing UEFA's backside.

Maybe. The reality may lie in simple logistics though. FA Cup tickets tend to be cheaper, the matches are at the weekend, often at 3pm on a Saturday, and probably not televised. But let me dream of more noble reasons, if only for a few minutes.

Milk Cup

This year, the League Cup is called the Carling Cup, and City ease through with a 2-0 win over Birmingham, and soon after put five past Wolverhampton Wanderers, as they beat them twice in a week. I have often wondered if sponsorships work in football. I am not a lager drinker, but if I was, and had low standards, am I really more likely to drink Carling because they sponsor a cup competition? I guess some people must be, or they wouldn't do it.

The only way I have seen the effectiveness of football sponsorship deals is in a negative way, due to the extreme pettiness football fans are capable of. I think twice before purchasing any red clothing, and I know fellow City fans who will never touch a product made by Sharp because they used to sponsor United. Cutting off your nose to spite your face. Football fans are rarely rational.

Elsewhere, I'm beginning to understand Twitter better. It's the online version of venting your spleen at a match. City beat Everton 2-0, but before that drop their first points of the season, letting a two-goal lead slip at Fulham. My timeline on Twitter would have you believe the club had just gone into administration after relegation. Yet I keep scrolling, with no idea of why, or what, I expect to find.

I'm trapped.

Home Time

I'm thinking about my dad on the tram home. He'd have loved today. He had - has - a long and consistent hatred of Everton, which stemmed from a hail of golf balls being lobbed his way across Stanley Park in the 1970s. To "get one over them" as he always called it would have given him great satisfaction. I can't wait to tell him about the match, for what it's worth. I take him a programme for every home game too, and write the score on the front. Just maybe it helps him a little. I hope so.

They are so much bulkier than they used to be, a proper read, with a price to match. At home I have a framed copy of the 1956 FA Cup Final match programme, the game where Bert Trautmann broke his neck and carried on playing, on a wall in the hall. It would be exaggerating to call it a pamphlet.

The Despair

Next up is the Champions League again, and what will surely be City's toughest match of the Group Stage, Bayern Munich away, against a team referred to as European royalty. Translation: their team is really good. The tie turns into a demoralising night, for numerous reasons. City lose 2-0, which is naturally disappointing. The real story is off the pitch though, as substitute Carlos Tevez refuses to come on, after seemingly getting annoyed at being asked to warm up multiple times and being overlooked in favour of a defensive substitute five minutes previous.

Ultimately, I'm annoyed because it is all so unnecessary. This nonsense will disrupt City's season, make them weaker and could ultimately cost the side dearly. And for what? City are not supposed to be inept anymore, garnering sympathy from other fans. I don't want to be that club anymore. But it seems some of the old ability of my club to shoot itself in the foot remains - the need to make life more difficult than at first seemed possible. If City don't qualify from their group, then fair enough. There will be criticism, and I can handle that. But this? This adds embarrassment into the mix.

I'm also annoyed because once more we are all talking about something that happened off the pitch. I seem to spend much of my time doing that nowadays. Ownership models, net spends, Financial Fair Play (whatever that is), ticket prices, atmospheres, racism, corruption and now a bust up on the touchline during an important Champions League game. I've waited so long for my club to be duking it out with Europe's elite sides, and now it's turning into a debacle.

So who is to blame? Two fiery characters clash, and this is the consequence. I guess blame therefore should be shared, and it is damage that can easily be repaired, but the initial noises from both camps make this very unlikely. Tevez must take more of the blame though, as he should do what his manager requests. If you are told to warm up, you warm up. And the big issue now is that this incident has ramifications far beyond the Champions League. Roberto Mancini strikes me as a man to hold grudges – or to rephrase that, one who does not forgive easily, and after the match he indicates he never wants to see Tevez again in a City shirt. This is bad news all round.

Behind the scenes, a different version of events soon arises - Mancini is quite willing to let Tevez back into the fold. Unfortunately, there is a caveat. Tevez must apologise to his teammates, which he refuses to do. The club suspend him without pay, and the Argentinean is soon trying to engineer a move away from the club. One of those badly-scrawled banners appears in the away end as City travel to Ewood Park a few days later, stating "Tevez Out", but I cannot agree, as we need him, and that feels more important than taking a stand against a disruptive player.

I need a distraction, so tune in to the North London derby, which Spurs win with a rare long-distance howitzer from Kyle Walker. Good player.

Thoughts Of An Insomniac

It's 2am and I can hear a dog barking. There is a full moon and it looks beautiful, and I can hear the distant hum of the boiler. I start typing again as I have thoughts to express. The tap tap on the keyboard may make me sleepy, hopefully.

The events in Munich highlight how substitutions are not necessarily all they seem. Carlos Tevez was upset because at 2-0 down, Roberto Mancini decided to make a defensive substitution, rather than use Tevez to try and get back into the game. On the surface, bringing on a defensive player when your team is trailing seems nonsensical. But was it on this occasion? Because if a manager brings on a defensive player but pushes two other players up the pitch, is the move defensive? No. And if a manager brings on a defensive player as a precursor to bringing on a striker, then suddenly there is more logic to the move. You get the feeling Carlos Tevez is not big on nuance though.

It's all done now, no going back. And after such a disappointing result, I often feel the need for another match as soon as possible, a palette cleanser, an opportunity to put right previous wrongs, the opposite to the old days, when I wanted a month between matches as I couldn't take much more punishment. Sadly, this is not an option, as what follows is the season's first international break. Looks like I'll be alone with my own thoughts for the next fortnight. I can't wait.

Sergio, Sergio....

Signings are symbolic. They can offer an insight into what the future holds, on and off the pitch, and signing Sergio Aguero was the perfect example of this. His importance to City lies not just in the goals he scores, or the success he creates. The fact he is at City gives me hope about what the future holds - because one of the best young strikers in the world needs to be persuaded to join a club with no recent record of success, and money alone won't be enough. After all, he would have got plenty of that that wherever he went. No, he is proof that my club's owners are serious about building something special. Whenever a club signs a player you thought they could not get, it feels like the club is going in the right direction. Though as any fan knows, it doesn't always turn out that way. Maybe they're hiding some nasty secrets instead, damaged goods.

Players have different reasons for joining a club. It is just a job for some of them, and that should not be forgotten. Money may be a motive. Family may be a factor, such as living in an area that is preferable for partners, their children and others. But for many of the best players, ambition drives their decision-making. That's why in a previous transfer window, City took a serious gamble that paid off spectacularly. Keen to sign Yaya Toure and David Silva, but wary that they needed significant persuasive powers to get them to Manchester, those in charge of negotiations at the club told Yaya Toure that David Silva had already agreed to join City (he had not), and told David Silva that Yaya Toure had agreed to join the club (he had not). Convinced that the other signing was a sign of the club's ambition, they both agreed to the move.

Players like Aguero, Toure and Silva, all previously used to Spanish climes, feed into my many insecurities. There is a theory held (perhaps just by me) that northern clubs are at a disadvantage in attracting top class players as London and surrounding areas are thought to be more desirable places to live. I'm not sure if that is true, but every time Manchester has a bout of bad weather, and there have been many, I getting this nagging concern at the back of my mind that the City players who grew up in warmer climes may be questioning their commitment to a Mancunian lifestyle. I question it on a weekly basis, so they must be.

Time With Dad

"I read the match programme you bought."

"Oh really? That's great."

"They're like a small book nowadays."

"Yes, plenty to look at."

"I hate Everton."

"Yes, I know. Well, we beat them 2-0."

"Good. Wish it had been ten."

"Did you see the article on Howard Kendall?"

"Good manager, but he left us in the lurch. Traitor."

"Well indeed."

"Liked a drink."

"Don't we all?"

"Can I have an orange juice?"

"Yes, of course."

Dad doesn't understand the concept of tribalism. When he was young, if United were at home that weekend, he'd occasionally go and see them instead of City. There may have been a rivalry, but the vitriol that rules in modern football was absent. We sat in the home's lounge one sunny day last year, on the anniversary of the Munich Air Tragedy. He talked of the great loss to the city as a whole, of the wonderful players lost to the world, and those that were never the same. He talked with awe about the likes of Frank Swift and Bert Trautmann before him. Bert would never be accepted in the modern world, my dad argued. Dad has a soft spot for keepers, as he was a handy one himself in his youth, as am I. I couldn't deal with the mental toughness to play that position though, the responsibility as the last line of defence would overwhelm me.

Tribalism is weird. Those not into sport don't understand it, but how could they? It makes no sense, really. As fans we take credit for our club's fortunes, as if we are responsible for them. A good atmosphere may spur on a team, but our influence on results is minimal. It's not really our glory to boast about. And it's not for us to stick up for or defend the dirtier, more unsavoury aspects of the beautiful game. It's just this thing we follow that affects our mood every single week, and there's nothing we can do about it. Once you're in, you're in. Committed to this life, and its ups and downs. Committed to the good players, the bad, the leaching owners or the perfect chairman.

My team is better than your team. My club is bigger than your club.

My.

Is the club mine? In a way, yes. But I don't get to take the credit for its achievements. I will, but I shouldn't.

Fuelled By Hate

I began to wonder if I hated Everton too, then I realised I find it hard to wish well on any football team, and that's not a good look. Hey, it is what it is. I theorise in my mind that the thought of other fans having success creates envy and jealousy, and perhaps it's not actually a hatred of the club or its fans that is the issue. But then I do find it every easy to hate on a club, and that is damning about how football has changed amongst its fans, as I know I am not alone in thinking this way. Everton fans seem to think that every decision that goes against them at Goodison is a miscarriage of justice. And they beat us quite a lot. I am compelled to hate Manchester United, for obvious reasons. I could go on for hours, from fanbases living in the past, to those with a deeply racist minority, to simply hating a fanbase because they celebrated City getting relegated. I'm looking at you, Ipswich Town, and I sincerely hope you experience 27 successive relegations. I work with someone who hates Preston because he once got food poisoning from a burger he ate outside Deepdale. My cousin doesn't like Middlesbrough because they postponed a match due to fog when he was a good three hours into his coach trip to Ayresome Park. No one can hold a grudge like a football fan.

There is a separate list though. This is the list of teams who are on the naughty step because they have single-handedly ruined betting accumulators. I despise Coventry City because they have ruined three separate accumulators in a single season. Birmingham City cannot be trusted. Nor Wycombe Wanderers. Basically, most clubs are on the list. All the teams I have cursed, who have become world-beaters the first time I back their opponents, and turn into pub teams when I back them. A new season brings a clean slate, but many of the same suspects will soon be back on the list.

Nevertheless, when they do come in, it's a buzz, which is why gambling is so dangerous in first place, hence why I limit myself to a £5 accumulator most Saturdays. I was once out with friends, and the bounce in my step led them to suggest I had clearly "got lucky" the previous night. I didn't think it was worth correcting them, my upbeat mood the result of a 94th minute goal from Accrington Stanley that won me £175. I preferred their story, just.

Gamble Responsibly

Those wins are rare. For me, at least.

I feel irritated, then I realise why. Good news for friends should be considered good news for me. After all, I want my friends to be happy. I am not a sociopath, to the best of my knowledge. Then I work it out. It is because my friend has won on his football accumulator, for the third time in a month. And I have not won one in almost a year. And I begrudge him this luck, it seems. Which makes me feel worse about myself. Better he has the money than a bookmaker, though friends never seem so keen to tell me about their losing accumulators. I wonder how many of them he has had in the past month?

The weekend accumulator is one of the group's traditions, and about half of us participate. I place all my bets online. Some friends like to go into a shop, and feel the thrill of picking up winnings. For me, there is a strict rule. A maximum of £10 per week, nothing more. I do not have an addictive personality, except when it comes to maize snacks, and know to keep this tradition cheap. I can afford to lose the price of a pint. If I win, I can bet again.

A 5:30pm Saturday home match is the perfect situation for an accumulator bet. 3pm arrives, and we get to live out our mostly failed bets together. All hoping for that exclamation at 4:20pm that "I just need Carlisle to score", followed by the dwindling hope as the clock ticks down.

EN-GER-LUND

I use the break to work my way through the back catalogue of Grandaddy, read some books, as I have been meaning to for some time, and clean the flat as I host a rare dinner party for friends. By dinner party, I mean I cook some food and we get drunk.

Part of me likes international breaks. Fandom is stressful, on and off the pitch. Everything you read in whatever this turns out to be will confirm this to you, that my fandom seems to consist of one near-breakdown after another. International breaks are often a joke, and badly timed, but they are a nice opportunity for a time-out from the day-to-day stresses of club football, where there is a period of mourning when a game is lost.

But internationals are troublesome, as players get ground into dust. It seems harder and harder for such players to have long, largely injury-free careers, as those who run the game seem less and less concerned about their welfare, and paying them a lot doesn't alter that. Players are *carbon footprinting* their way around the globe, but the honest truth is I am less concerned about the impending and perhaps inevitable destruction of our planet, and more that Edin Dzeko might be a bit leggy for Norwich at home.

But in the end, perhaps the greatest gift international breaks can give us is reminding us of why we love club football so much. A palette cleanser before footballers get back to the real business. Qualifiers are like the Champions league group stage for the best teams. They have their moments, but essentially it's just a warm up for the real excitement. Qualifying used to be an intermittent problem for England, but nowadays there is little jeopardy. And with the talent coming through, that is unlikely to change in the years ahead.

I reckon too, without any evidence to back it up, that England means more to fans who supports clubs that never win anything, as it is their best chance to experience glory as a football fan, at least at the top level. Don't get me wrong, a promotion means as much to a Barnsley fan as a Premier League title win for City would mean to me, should it ever happen. But you will see from the flags of many fans that those of what are considered "smaller clubs" like to follow the national side, from many sides that rarely get the buzz of glory provided by their club. Once, that was me, and I pined for some form of glory from my national side.

Anyway, I use the second half of the break as a reason to get on a plane and visit a distant friend. Someone I went to school with, who is doing very well for himself, but doesn't make me feel bad about it. And I am glad there is no club football during my time away. I've seen many a City game on foreign shores, and I don't need the pressure of my day being made or ruined by a result. In international week, I can sit in a bar in shorts watching football, without the stress.

I look forward to watching England not because they are my everything, but because of the exact opposite of that. I don't care enough to allow their results to send me into a slump. Now don't get me wrong, I am an England supporter, and I want them to succeed. It's just that it can never mean even a quarter, no a tenth, as much as my club means to me. There is no comparison. When it comes to football, it's club over country every time. I would rather my club won an FA Cup than England win the World Cup. Though it would be even better if both happened.

Nevertheless, there is much to be gained from international football. There is something wonderful when the England team does play well, and the country feels like it is united. There is something deeply marvellous about the finals of competitions, period. They present an opportunity to type my favourite word, as finals bring with them a smorgasbord of football, day-in, day-out. Falling behind on work because Denmark v Chile is on the BBC at 2pm. Added interest if there's a few Premier League players scattered across the two squads. I think back to Euro 96, and I recall my national side's performances being an integral part of one of my favourite summers. I was living in Leeds at the time, having decided that a change of scenery would help focus my mind and get my life back on track. It didn't, but I still enjoyed my two years there. And that summer felt amazing. The sun was out, there was a buzz in the air about football coming home, and I felt great. Naturally football has a unique ability to send you crashing back down to earth, as do Germany in a penalty shootout, but my memories remain fond.

I flitted between Manchester and Leeds that summer. On the morning of the England v Scotland game, I sat in my parents' back garden, as the sun shone fiercely, determined to finally rid myself of my pallid appearance, before heading into the centre of Manchester to watch the match in the afternoon. I have a vivid recollection of hearing a strange banging noise, as I sat five miles north of the centre, as if something had fallen off the back of a lorry at the front of the house. What had actually happened was the IRA had detonated a bomb that decimated part of Manchester's city centre. And I remember watching England v Scotland that afternoon in a local pub instead, a feeling of shock still rushing through me in waves.

Sadly, my own experiences have rather tempered my enthusiasm for England. The problems of England fans abroad is well-documented. In November 2007, I went to Wembley to see England there for the first time. And perhaps the last. I should not let a single night cloud my opinion of a team, because if I did, I would have given up on Manchester City before the end of the 1980s. But it was one of those nights where everything went wrong. England needed to avoid defeat to qualify for Euro 2008. The weather was terrible, and so were England. There was barely concealed racism around me, mostly delivered in a local accent. The rain never stopped and England lost, so would not be at the following summer's finals. Our hotel was a way from Watford station, after the tedious journey to get there, so we were soaked to the skin, and I was forced to sleep on the floor as there were only two beds for four of us.

The next morning, exhausted but hungry, I demolished a full English breakfast in Wetherspoons, as the TV screen filled with news that Steve McClaren had been sacked as England manager. Never again, I vowed to myself. Something had changed.

There are other reasons for this apathy. I used to feel inordinate pride at the possibility of a City player representing England. Now it feels like rival fans are waiting for a reason to criticise them when they pull on the shirt. It's hard work. Manchester United fans have been derided for years for chanting "Argentina" in honour of their players who were born there, rather than supporting England, and I used to be one of the people deriding them. I now understand, and have begun to see the wider picture. I've seen City players slated repeatedly when representing England not because they were the worst player, but because they play for City. What's more, patriotism, or pride in your own country, does not have to be represented by singing the national anthem loudly, waving flags, or by zealously supporting a football team. And yet there are millions in England who do think they are the sole criteria.

England fans are made up of all shapes, sizes and characters, so I should not really focus on the minority who can spoil it for the rest. But it is hard at times to be enthusiastic about my national team with all that surrounds them, a situation that is exacerbated when the big games draw close. The barely concealed xenophobia and the harking back to 1966 that much of the media love to participate in is odious and demoralising, and has only served to strengthen my resolve to stick to club football, as far as live football is concerned.

The Wider World

City beat Aston Villa 4-1. But naturally that's not the main talking point around the water coolers of the world. The news is dominated by the death of Colonel Muammar Muhammad Abu Minyar al-Gaddafi. I've no idea what I am supposed to do with this news. Is it good? Is it bad? How do you rationalise such an event?

World events may provide me with perspective regarding the main love of my life. After all, something I often take for granted, my health and the health of those around me, is far more important than any football result. There are things going on in the world with real consequences that effect millions, that goes well beyond me feeling a bit down because we've been knocked out of the FA Cup. But it's OK to care about your football team, even if it feels overpowering sometimes. And I can't just switch off anyway, so even if it wasn't OK, there's nothing I can do about it. Sport has its place in history too. Football has caused wars, saved lives, changed a country's outlook. It matters, and it is fine to say so.

The city I grew up in and call my own, played a big part in modern football's emergence, and its importance in many of our lives. That's because Manchester was once dubbed Cottonopolis because of its integral role in the Industrial Revolution of the 19th century – and the Industrial Revolution gave birth to modern football.

Small, provincial industrial towns produced the first successful football teams because the sport flourished in towns with migrant workers who came from across the continent to work in the factories. They were in an imposing new town, and often could not speak the language, and had few friends to speak of. Football gave such people a sense of belonging, and something to be passionate about. Like it does to this day, it brought people together. Football began to reflect society. It became an outlet for passion, frustration, and of course violence and hooliganism.

Anyway, enough history lessons.

There is a cloud on the horizon.

Next up is the Manchester Derby.

"At the moment we have a neighbour and sometimes neighbours are noisy."
Alex Ferguson, September 2009

Derby Day.

I hate it.

I hate the build-up, I hate the day itself, I hate the tension, nerves, the thought of losing to THEM. If I could sleep through every Derby Day, I would. And yet the previous season provided one of the greatest days for my club, with a Derby win at Wembley, so perhaps cowards like me need to get a grip. I cannot change though. It is who I am. As usual the build-up is dominated by ex-players, mainly from the red side, bigging up their team and belittling the opposition. Boring fayre, but easy content for the newspapers.

Some losses matter more than others, and the more that is at risk, the more the nerves are ramped up. It took me a long time to realise "bragging rights" are overrated, as they are so fleeting. They count for little as football moves on quickly, and the next game needs to be won just as much. Every time I see someone say "Manchester is red" or "Manchester is blue" a little of me dies. But nevertheless, even an end-of-season Derby with little on the line is enough to activate my anxiety rashes. It is ingrained in all football fans that a Derby matters, that honour is at stake, and that defeat is too painful for words. It is why I am glad when it is over. And why for the week leading up to such a match, I am not at my best, whatever my best may be. Part of the problem is that some people, weirdos, actually like matches like this, and relish the occasion, as I find out at work during the week before the match. They want to talk about the match, and I want to talk about anything else.

Hating Derby Days is a natural bed fellow for my psyche. When I broke up with Claire, a mutual decision she suggested, I accepted my fate. I have always just accepted things that happen, without fighting for something different. I am not a risk-taker. I seek an easy life, one devoid of problems, obstacles, or disappointment. Take the badly-paid but non-stressful job. Avoid confrontation. Do not relish big football matches, because the thought of losing scares you, even though the rewards are so much greater.

City have beaten United a few times in recent years, but always as the underdog. At last, they get to play United as equals, which simply makes me even more nervous, as expectations are higher. Heroic defeats are no longer sufficient. The only acceptable result is a win, though as with any Derby Day, a draw is good enough, as it keeps away the gut-wrenching bad mood that inevitably follows defeat. For this reason, I would happily take an endless run of draws for the rest of my life.

Comeback Kings

In February 2004, Manchester City travelled to Tottenham Hotspur for an FA Cup replay. It didn't go particularly well for City in the first half, to put it mildly. They went three goals down and to make matters worse, somehow, Joey Barton got himself sent off as the teams walked off the pitch at half-time. Game over, in the most miserable fashion possible.

Or not, as it turned out. In one of the great FA Cup comebacks, City scored four goals in the 2nd half, including a late headed winner from Jon Macken. This match was not televised, but it was such a historic feat that the BBC cleared their schedule to broadcast an impromptu Match Of The Day.

I was naturally euphoric at the performance, barely believing what had just happened. Yet at the back of my mind, some seeds of doubt. Despite a win that would go down in history, I had this nagging voice in my head. Why?

Well, the draw for the next round had already been made. And the winners of this tie would play Manchester United, at Old Trafford.

Another Derby, which City were likely to lose. Which they did.

Match Day

By the end of the season's first derby, all those fears are washed away.

Final score at Old Trafford – Manchester United 1 Manchester City 6.

What a game. A strange one in many ways. City do not dominate the first half, but find themselves ahead at the break due to a sublime Mario Balotelli finish. After scoring, Balotelli lifts his shirt to reveal a T-shirt on which is written "Why Always Me?". A deeply philosophical question, that I assume relates to his media treatment.

Early in the 2nd half, United are down to ten men, and City take over. They go three up, but with ten minutes to go, United get a goal back, and naturally I start panicking. Thankfully, City keep United at arm's length with ease, and late on everything stops making sense. City add three more goals, spurning two great chances in the process. Amidst the carnage, David Silva assists an Edin Dzeko goal with one of the greatest passes I have ever seen. It will be replayed in 50 years' time, I swear. It is a rout, humiliating for the home side, and one of the greatest score lines I have ever witnessed, surpassing the 5-1 derby win of 1989. This is hard to take in, impossible to process. Little old City have just put six goals past their behemoth of a rival. Seismic, as one newspaper described it the following day.

Falling In Love Again

Sometimes, it can be a little thing that makes you go from liking a footballer or manager to loving them, and towards the end of this match, I fall in love with Roberto Mancini. I finally put a ring on it. The camera switches to him sat in the dugout with the rout complete, and he looks as dashing as ever, wearing a City scarf with real panache, but that misses the point. He is sat there, chuckling away, incredulous at what had just happened. It felt like he was one of us. And he was changing the psyche of my football club and that meant changing the psyche of the fan base.

The rest of the day is a blur. I drink until I can drink no more. There is nothing that can wipe the smile off my face. The next morning I wake up on the couch, with half a pizza millimetres away. My head hurts, but I feel great, because a good win is almost as much about the next day as the match itself.

Social media can be fun, I now realise that - when results go your way, funnily enough. A photo of a sick swan is trending, because of the score line. I'm sure you can work out why.

Thoughts Of An Insomniac

Not that I slept all night. A thought pops into my head that literally awakens me at 3am. Sleeping with alcohol in my system is always fitful at best. This result means very little if City do not now win the league. Yes, there has to be a negative in all of this, I cannot change old habits just yet. But there is certainly a logic in my thought process. That result will remain in the history books, and the memory of the day itself and the joy it brought, for many weeks thereafter, cannot be extinguished. But its importance is amplified if it is part of a title-winning campaign. And whilst City went into the game as league leaders, this match has caused a seismic shift in expectations. Now City are not a team that could win the Premier League, but are a team that are now expected to win it.

With this in mind, a philosophical debate lingers in my head for a few days about whether future events can tarnish a big result. That 6-1 win happened, and nothing can change that. Perhaps I should accept it for what it is. Or perhaps I should compromise and agree on the following: the result will always be historic, and nothing can take away from that, but if City go on to win the league, then it gets to take on even greater significance. Especially if the title race is a tight one.

Dad Time

I go and see dad, to talk about the amazing game at Old Trafford. A chant soon starts up at City matches: "It should have been ten". That may be a bit of hyperbole, but it gets me looking to the past again.

I've seen my team score ten goals, in 1987 against Huddersfield Town. It finished 10-1, with three separate hat-trick scorers. My dad insists that at full time a player kicked the ball into the crowd at full-time, and he caught it, then threw it back. I am not sure of the veracity of such claims, but I do recall that Huddersfield were the better side for the first 20 minutes.

Their solitary goal was from a penalty at 9-0, and it was a terrible decision by the referee.

The Real Thing

Now we will see what they are made of, as the pressure is now truly on. Three more league wins follow, and City are well clear at the top of the table. They have started conceding a few goals, but are still scoring for fun.

This is all new, competing for a league title. It requires a different mentality, as the spotlight is on the club far more than would be for a promotion push. If it feels pressured for the fans, it must be doubly so for the players, many of whom are also experiencing their first title challenge at such a level. How they cope with the pressure may well determine how the season pans out. But this result has made it crystal clear – City are title challengers. My team, going for a Premier League title. Might even be first on Match of the Day, or part of Sky's Super Sunday line up. One of the big boys.

On the downside, City's ownership model, and where the money comes from, is subject to far more scrutiny, and has been for at least a year now.

Football fans and most of the media do not care too much about how clubs are funded until said club starts becoming successful, when suddenly it is an issue. Even more so if that club threatens the established status quo, who swathes of the media have spent their lives worshipping. Look at me, getting all paranoid. I guess City really have arrived.

I'm A Coward

You have to be brave to go to big away games. Now I'm not comparing such supporters to soldiers in a war zone. But consider this – I have never watched City at Old Trafford in a competitive game. Because I'm a coward, for the second time in this tome. It will not be the last time. I assure you. Watching my team lose, live, is never fun, but the thought of losing in United's stadium fills me with dread, as it should. But really, that should not stop me going, if I could get a ticket. But I have never gone, as I have always expected the worse, often with good reason. As already mentioned, I'd be happy to hide in a cupboard every Derby Day. Perhaps my attitude will change in time, now that City can walk onto the pitch as equals. Maybe one day, hopefully, United fans will be filled with that same existential dread. And the upside, seeing City triumph at their main rivals' ground, surely makes it a risk worth taking? After the 1-6 win, I am euphoric, but am also filled with envy for those blues that experienced it live.

I have been to Old Trafford a few times. I went to see City play United in Denis Irwin's testimonial, which was a feisty affair, but not one that mattered. City lost, and I have vague memories of George Weah injuring Irwin with a late tackle. This testimonial was played mid-season for some reason, making Irwin a doubt for their next game. I saw Argentina draw with Russia in 1991 in the England Challenge Cup. And I was there when David Beckham curled in a late free-kick against Greece in 2001 that saw England qualify for the World Cup. Putting my prejudices to one side, Beckham was amazing that day, though I recall him having plenty of wild free-kicks that afternoon before one finally went in, in the nick of time.

But to watch City in a competitive match? No, it has never happened. And for choosing to watch Derbies cowering behind a couch, I have now paid the price, and missed out on an experience that those there will cherish forever. Sometimes you have to take a gamble in life, beyond a £5 accumulator.

Back In The Office

"Have you got the figures for the car insurance take up this month?"

"Yeah, I'll email them to you in a minute if that's OK?"

"Yeah that's fine."

"Anything else you need?"

"No."

"OK."

You not going to say it then?"

"Say what?"

"Oh come on."

"What? I've no idea what you're talking about."

"Yeah, course you don't."

"Seriously, I've no idea what you are getting at."

"Just get it over with. Come on, slag off United. I can take it."

"Oh, the football? United losing 6-1 at home in a Derby? Just assumed you wouldn't want to talk about it."

"Well, maybe I do."

"Ah right. Well, to be honest, I don't. Just another win really."

"Just another win?!"

"Yeah, three points is three points at the end of the day."

"This is a wind up. You're winding me up. Fuck this."

"Eh? Ah don't be like that Joe, I am being serious..... ah, he's gone. Shame."

Fireworks

After the match, news emerges that Mario Balotelli destroyed much of his house by letting off fireworks the night before the Derby. Just another Mario Balotelli story. Here is a young guy that clearly seems to struggle with boredom, with sometimes catastrophic results. Who knows if the story is even true, as there is a whole industry devoted to fabricating tales of what Mario gets up to. But his house has definitely been damaged by fire, so this looks like a more reliable rumour. How do you deal with characters like Mario Balotelli, as a manager? An arm round the shoulder, or an icy Mancini stare? A bit of both I imagine. A reminder that being a manager is about more than tactics. You're a social worker, psychologist, media guru and a hundred other things.

Bragging Rights

Such a strange phrase that, isn't it? A theme I will repeatedly return to in this book, it begs the question – what are you bragging about?

To which the answer can only be: in the distant past I made a decision over which football team to support, though to be honest it may have been made for me, and right now that decision is working in my favour due to a specific result or set of results, and so I am puffing out my chest and taking credit for the actions of others, over which I had no influence whatsoever, and deriding those that made a decision earlier in life to support a different club, which my club has just defeated. My team is better than your team, and the more people that are made aware of this, the better. Worship at my feet, please.

The internet is the perfect place to brag. It's full of strutting peacocks. It has presented other opportunities to us all however, as I realise as my Twitter experience continues. With the rise of social media, opportunities have emerged for the "typical" fan. A chance to have a voice and your opinions heard, not that this is always a good thing. The downside for me if you choose to have that voice and commit to a public profile of sorts is that you essentially become a slave to fortune. You advertise your allegiance, which is fine when things are going well. But when they are not, and that time will always arrive at some point, then you are an obvious target, someone to be shot at. On Facebook, it's just people you know. Your allegiances are probably common knowledge. It's different on Twitter, where you project yourself to friends and strangers. My bio does rather give my allegiances away, however.

After City beat United, and then Stoke, to win the FA Cup, I wanted to shout from the rooftops. I wanted to rub it in with United fans, act as immaturely as possible as the adrenalin affected my judgement. Thankfully, I largely kept my counsel, because I know all too well what it feels like to be on the receiving end of such treatment - and what goes around, comes around.

Rivalries

By writing all these thoughts down, I am forced to repeatedly think about football and the stresses that come with it, plus the idea that much of the time football does not bring me joy, as it can be overbearing, when the essence of football is that it should be fun. Nothing encapsulates the ups and downs and almost schizophrenic nature of following a football team more than a big rivalry with another team.

Rivalries are weird, really weird. Another part of the sport that outsiders must look at and shake their heads with exasperation. The things we come out with, and the absolute certainty we have that what we say is 100% accurate. Rival fans are all idiots, biased and pathetic, whilst my fanbase is a class above, and far less embarrassing than THEM. But we believe we are fair and impartial with these views. I've seen a small but passionate sub-section spring up of fans who commit much of their time to slagging off their own fanbase, perhaps to prove to the world how impartial they are.

The best way to prove that being an impartial football fan is close to impossible would be to consider the views I would have if my dad was a United fan, and as a young child I had started supporting them instead. Can I really say that I would hold identical views about City and United fans if I had taken that different path? Of course not, I would hold totally different views, and would be expected to. We're all biased, and football feeds into humans' inherent tribalism, and we're all hypocrites too when it suits us. And to be honest, I wouldn't have it any other way.

I think about this as I read some nonsense opinion piece by a football journalist who I know to be a United fan, not that he would ever admit it. Journalists purport to be impartial, but they all support someone. If that team is in the same division as the other teams they cover as part of their job, then I fail to see how 100% impartiality is possible. I've heard fans accuse some journalists of being little more than fanzine writers, pandering to a single fanbase, telling them what they want to hear. That's incredibly harsh on fanzines, who have produced some of the best football content around for many years – and often with far more critical and balanced content than you will see in a newspaper.

The only people involved in football that can ignore their favourite club are the players themselves. If we agree that everyone falls in love with football via a single club, players have a reason to break away from the hold a club has on us fans. If you play for Aston Villa but supported West Bromwich Albion as a child, it is easier to dedicate yourself to the success of Villa, as you are more involved. You have a say in their fortune.

Back In The Pub

Ste suggests a drink one night at our local, and the United game is on the TV in the corner.

"If I had the power to relegate United to the third tier of English football, would you tell me to use that power?"
"Well yeah, obviously."
"But why?"
"Because life would be so much easier without the rivalry."
"I'm not so sure. I mean I hate Derby Day so much, on the surface the idea of never having to play United sounds like paradise. But I'm not sure it would be."
"Depends if the rivalry gives you more good days than bad, I guess."
"I'll always remember my United-supporting friend telling me that he missed the rivalry with City."
"Wonder if he regrets that now?"
"A bit perhaps. But without a local rival, that semi-final victory last season doesn't exist, the 6-1 this season is not a thing, the 5-1 too. Would you rather we won 3-0 v Bolton instead?"
"I'd rather not have experienced the many defeats, watching them win hundreds of trophies or the pity that rained down on us for two decades. They feel like Pyrrhic victories."
"But if we are properly good now, permanently, we can change that. No victory feels better than beating them. Life's richer with a rivalry. A proper one. And if we win the league this season…"
"And if we don't…"

Image Is Everything

There is a reason that image of Roberto Mancini laughing in the dugout is still so vivid in my mind. It's because when the 6th goal went in I did the same. I did not celebrate – I laughed, at the absurdity of it all.

Would it have meant as much to see Mark Hughes sat there laughing? I'd have loved it, but there is something about Mancini, that shows that some managers are just treated and perceived differently. We form opinions and develop prejudices from very little. How people look, how they speak, their demeanour. Roberto Mancini exudes an air of calm chic, but it is believed that his public persona is much different to that behind the scenes. He is exact, a perfectionist, demanding and confrontational at times. A religious man, he considers the colour purple unlucky, for reasons unknown. He sees injuries as a sign of weakness. He demands dedication from his players. And so far, he seems to be getting it. And he is getting respect from the wider football circle.

Most fans won't know about any of this though. They will just see the attractive, debonair Italian on the touchline, a man who demands your attention. If I was a City player, I'd be keen to impress. As an aside, he is also a man who would look sexy wearing a bin bag. It's very annoying.

Mancini knows his football, and has got his team playing exciting, attacking football. The team is well organised, the squad talented and varied. But as a manager you need more, you need that favourable perception. If journalists are writing nice things about you, players are more likely to toe the line. The old school of English managers – your Harry Redknapps, your Sam Allardyces, love to moan about how they would get more respect and bigger jobs if they had a Spanish or Italian name. This is of course nonsense, overlooking the possibility that they may not be good enough to warrant bigger jobs. After all, how many chairmen care about nationality? They just want success. Nevertheless, there is something about someone like Roberto Mancini that allows him to woo and seduce not just a singular fanbase, but much of the football media too. Ultimately, this will count for little if results do not follow. But it always helps a manager to have the press on your side.

Mancini certainly did not have the press on his side initially. The main reason for that was due to him replacing a sacked British manager, a cardinal sin at many a tabloid sports desk. Mark Hughes has his friends in the media, as many of his ilk do. He did an OK job at City, but nothing more. After the takeover, City's owner and the board gave him a chance to prove himself, and he didn't take that chance. So he was replaced, after a run of dropped points and underwhelming performances. That is football, an occurrence that happens repeatedly every season, in every league. But for Hughes supporters, the dismissal was unacceptable. They were furious, his sacking representing everything wrong with football. Game's gone, hasn't it? One journalist even fabricated a story of how Mancini was in the stands during Hughes' last home game. Fortunately, it soon became clear Mancini was not one to give too much attention to his portrayal. He had a job to do, and that is precisely what he is doing.

Heroes

I am walking through town and I see Roberto Mancini outside a restaurant, on his phone. Sorting a deal, perhaps. I smile and nod as I pass him, as if we're old acquaintances, and this is a common experience, like walking past a colleague in the office. He does not notice me, but it has still made my day. My life is not very exciting.

I have met four City managers in my time. Sven Goran appears a dour unassuming man on the surface, the sort of person you could easily imagine working as a sales manager for a paper clip company, but in reality a man who can seduce and impregnate you with a single handshake. Stuart Pearce was a decent bloke, as is Joe Royle. Just meeting the man who is managing or has ever managed my football club is deeply satisfying. Whether they were good or bad at it, they have done something rather special, in my eyes.

The Path I Took

How did I get to this point, my team in a title race, me typing my every thought into Microsoft Word, celebrating putting six goals past our biggest rivals, on their patch?

When I was barely two years old, my dad took me to City, and that was that. Well, not really, I wasn't aware what on earth was going on. We visited other grounds together, but Maine Road was where we both settled. My dad supported City, so going elsewhere occasionally made little sense. Soon I understood my surroundings, and the deal was done. I was a City fan, and would remain so. Does that make football similar to religion? In a way, but it's probably easier to change your religion than change football team. Dad doesn't remember what my first game was, though he thinks we were playing a team in red or white. He remembers his own first game, a 4-1 win at home to Newcastle United just before the Second World War. City were in the 2nd division at the time, and soon the league programme would be suspended, with the players' contracts terminated. Many joined the armed services, though a War League was later formed to keep the population entertained.

We did not have season tickets, so my attendance was sporadic, on average attending half the home games in any given season. This number increased if City showed the slightest signs of improvement. With no season tickets tying us to one spot, we moved around the ground. Occasionally taking in the heaving terrace on the Kippax, once I was old enough, and thus tall enough, to see any of the action. And a few times before then too, if memory serves. Dad had to hold me up, though just being there was often enough for me, my senses overloaded. I looked up to dad, in every sense of the word. Sometimes my dad preferred a sit down, so we would reside in the Main Stand, beneath its eclectic cantilever roof, and I would stare across at the Kippax, pining. That's where most of the noise and the character was, that's where I felt most alive. Sometimes we would sit behind a goal, but I preferred to be down the side of the pitch, the opposite of what I feel now. I struggled with perspective at the far end if I was behind the nets. Night matches had an extra thrill because dad would take me to the chippy before the match, as long as I didn't tell mum. There was no chance of that happening. Sausage, chips and gravy. The salt in the chippy was always better, and I never worked out why. Size of the grains said my dad, which seemed as good a reason as any. He would have a scallop too, and always do the same joke of trying to force a bit into my mouth, as he knew I hated them.

When I was 15, my dad had a heart attack, which I was convinced was because of all the "scraps" he had with his chippy teas. He survived, and I remember the doctor telling him he could live a long and prosperous life if he improved his diet. Mum banned butter from the house, and cream cakes too. Salads were introduced, which almost sent dad into a spiral of depression. My parents would go for walks in Heaton Park as part of his exercise regime. The only vice that remained, after a heated discussion, was our Saturday chippy lunch.

Dad was ordered to coalesce, so going to watch City was off the table. It was not good for his health at the best of times. This posed a problem for me, as I had no one to go with. And I knew my mum would not let me go by myself, so I did what any self-respecting teenager would do, and went without telling her, with an elaborate cover story about staying at a friend's house. I had to bribe my friend £3 to back me up should he ever be asked. And so I left the house with a ruck sack, which I immediately hid in a bush in the front garden. I got the 135 bus, then the 41, and used pocket money to cover the ticket price. And the weird thing was, I was nervous, really nervous. I had never been anywhere by myself, apart from school.

And I loved it. I felt liberated, on the terrace, free to stand where I wished. Free to shout what I wanted, free to concentrate on the football and the match day experience. It felt exhilarating, and City won comfortably, 3-1 against Luton Town, which helped. One of my favourite players, Ian Bishop, scored. Streaming out with the crowd at the end, I was reminded of the power of football. I felt like an adult for the first time, too.

I had enough change left for chips and gravy and a can of fizzy Vimto. I got the same buses back, got home at around 11pm, and with a straight face told my mum that my friend had got sick, so his mum dropped me back home. The first and perhaps only act of rebellion in my life. What a buzz. What a night.

The next morning, my mum bumped into my friend's mum in Tesco.
I was grounded for two months.

Back On The Pitch

In the middle of all this, City beat Villareal twice, including a last-gasp Sergio Aguero winner, to get their Champions League campaign back on track. I have still not worked out why teams play each other twice in succession in the middle of these group stages. Villareal were the team from Pot 2, but it has now become clear they are the whipping boys of the group. It is also clear that City and Napoli are fighting for the 2nd qualification place. The problem with whipping boys is that they don't pick up many points. The consequence of that is that City will need more points to qualify. If everyone beats Villareal, City's six points against them counts for much less.

Last-Gasp

Last-minute goals. Is there a better feeling than your team winning (or even avoiding defeat) with a late goal? The rush, the security of knowing there's little if any time for it to then go wrong. I walk away from the Villareal match on a bigger high than if City had won 3-0.

Think of some of the greatest matches of previous years and many of them involve a vital last-gasp goal. For some, this is a prerequisite for a classic match. From Michael Thomas winning Arsenal the league at Anfield in 1989, to Manchester United's Champions League victory in 1999. And later that week, my own team's history may have turned out very differently without Paul Dickov's late equaliser in the play-off final.

I Could Have Been A Contender

Work have sent me to a meeting in the depths of Lancashire. I have to give a 15-minute presentation on intranet updates, and then sit there bored for a further five hours or so. Thankfully, help is at hand. The conference room is at a small football ground, and overlooks a gleaming, pristine pitch. And as any fan knows, this gives me ample opportunity to pass time, as I day dream my way to the Ballon D'Or. For in my imagination, I can be whatever I want to be. The greatest keeper, the hat-trick hero. The world is my oyster. All you need for that imagination to run wild is some goal posts, and off you go. I sit there imagining overhead kicks, spectacular saves and last-ditch goal line clearances. There is nothing I cannot do.

As the hours of this tedious meeting pass by, and a discussion erupts over sales figures in the south-east, I think of the simple pleasures football provides. Walking out into an empty football stadium, for example when I did the stadium tour. The grass, the stands rising up above, the staff going about their daily business. Evocative. A football rolling towards you – this is your moment to shine. A ball rattling the underside of the bar. It's the sound, the thud, the vibration. All the better if it's been raining and the water is shaken off like a dog after exiting a river. Seeing a football stadium whilst on a foreign holiday. Mocking rival fans celebrating a goal that wasn't a goal, watching a centre back celebrate passionately, shots that go for throw ins, when the ball hits the corner flag and stays in, and so much more.

There is one more too....

Later that month I cycle past Old Trafford as a game is in progress. The outside of a ground during a match fascinates me. There is still a hive of activity, with vendors preparing for after the match, or packing up. It is dark now, so the glow from the ground illuminates the area. Then there is the noise. At times you would be hard-pushed to know there was a match taking place, but then an attack begins, and the volume is raised. Applause and chants break out sporadically. A fascinating soundtrack.

Jekyll And Hyde

Manchester United do not crumble after their Derby defeat, and it is clear they will not be fading away. There is one reason for this. Alex Ferguson is City fans' kryptonite, in that he has been the mastermind behind United's success for two decades. When he goes, United will be immediately weakened. It is thus natural to hate Ferguson, and to be fair he makes it quite easy much of the time, such is his autocratic rule at the club. I laugh at his fabled mind games, that if you believe what you read reduces opposition managers and players to drooling wrecks. What is without doubt though is his genius as a manager, though I was surprised to hear from a friend's father a few weeks ago, a lifelong season-ticket holder at Old Trafford, that he considers Ferguson overrated because he has only won the European Cup twice.

Managers like Ferguson, who come across as gruff and outright rude on match-day are often portrayed as lovely people away from the pressure of the day job. There are numerous managers I can think of that fit this category, who live Jekyll & Hyde lives. I'm reminded of this after City win at QPR, as their manager Neil Warnock gives his reaction to an exciting game. Warnock does his usual routine, the hard-luck story we know all too well, though on this occasion with some justification, as his side were excellent, and on another day would have picked up at least a point. But I really despise the way managers like him act to others in the sport. Their jobs are high pressure, and I can understand that it can affect how they act, and that marginal gains can make all the difference. But that is still no excuse for how some managers treat others. Warnock is from the school of managers whose team never deserves to lose a game, decry match officials relentlessly, and spend every minute of every match moaning and shouting at whoever is closest. He is also part of the "old-school" rota of British managers that will never be criticised widely for anything outside of results. They will call such actions necessary to eke out marginal gains, I would call it bullying. I can't wait for relics like him to be out of the game.

November 19th, 2011.

City beat Newcastle United 3-1 to remain at the top of the table. I'm happy with the result, but there is something else that consumes my thoughts for the rest of the day. Two seats from me sits a friend of a friend. I know him well enough to chat, but he's not someone I socialise much with, if ever. Truth is, if we never saw each other again, it wouldn't weigh heavily on my mind, and I am sure that feeling is mutual. We all know people like this. Acquaintances, brought together very occasionally as part of a crowd. Today however, this friend of a friend, becomes a much bigger part of my life, at least for a day.

City are playing quite well, and it is one of those games where the victory is functional. The team does not hit the heights but the superior quality of the eleven players is more than enough to win the game without moving into the high gears. There are a couple of players far from their peak however, and midway through the second half, Joleon Lescott misplaces a pass, and not for the first time. It is just after this moment that I think the guy two seats down says something racist.

I think.

But I am not certain. No one around me reacts as if anything has been said. Did I mishear? I was concentrating on the match after all. There is background noise, as always. But I know what I think I heard.

But I am not sure. I just cannot be certain. And if I was, what would I do at that moment? The second half progresses, City win, I go to the pub. But the incident that may or may not have happened weighs on my mind.

It plays on my mind that perhaps subconsciously I am convincing myself that I am not sure I heard what I suspect I heard. Because it is easier not to have heard, it is easier to turn a blind eye. And I do not want to be that person. I am damn sure this would never happen, but what if a close friend said something racist at a match? How would I react? What if it was a complete stranger? Should my reactions be different according to who made the comment? In an ideal world no, but I know that it may not play out that way. There is a lot swimming round my brain.

It's easy for me to look the other way, as a white male who has breezed through life due to an accident of birth. And deep down I know that ten years ago, I would definitely have looked the other way when certain of hearing abuse. But I hope I am a different person now. And that next time, if I know what I have heard, I am decisive in my actions, whoever said it.

I've been lucky in another way in that I have rarely heard racist abuse at a football match. The situation may be far better than twenty years ago, when bananas would be thrown onto pitches, but racists will always exist in all areas of society. And they go to football matches. Every fanbase has them, some more than others. All I can hope is that we move in the right direction and that there are fewer people like I was as a youngster, more than happy to look the other way.

Scapegoats

At least on the pitch, I have less to complain about. City fans used to love scapegoats. The football team wasn't very good much of the time, so it wasn't a difficult undertaking to identify one, or six, though we seemed as a fan base to have a preference for full backs. More on that in a minute. I don't need to name names. And scapegoats serve their purpose, distasteful as they are. When things are not going well, someone has to be to blame and focusing on the chairman gets boring after a while. Everything that happens in football must have blame attached to it – every goal for example is, for some, the result of sub-standard defending.

But things are going well at City, and for the first time in my life, there isn't a player getting stick, no one being singled out. Well, there's always someone, but it's much more low-key than in the past. There's a belief in the side, and it's a new sensation, after all these years.

City fans had a proud tradition of scapegoating full-backs during many of the club's leaner years. Maybe it was because the club made a succession of poor purchases in those positions. Or maybe as fans we underestimated, and still do, how difficult the full-back role is. I tried to argue this in the pub the other week, and whilst I got some agreement, I lost the crowd when I said strikers shouldn't cost more, as every position in a football team is as important as any other.

Round The Corner

You never know what is around the corner. I feel good. My football team are good, I have my health, friends, and enough money to live my life and cover the essentials. And then with one phone call, everything changes. My gran has died, aged 92. Peacefully, in her sleep, with no warning.

Polly was my mum's mum, and she certainly lived a full life. Evacuated from Warsaw in 1938, she flourished in post-war England by opening up a haberdashery shop that served as a focal point in the community, partly due to the fact that she loved to feed her customers as part of the service. She was full of life, and her presence filled any room. As a small child, I was scared of her intellect and wit, which I found intimidating. But with time, I grew to love these characteristics. And what was so important to me was that she had no interest in football, but she knew I did, and so it became important to her. She followed City results because she was invested in my happiness as she was with everyone she loved, and she understood implicitly the connection between the two. I was once at a family meal the day after a catastrophic and perhaps costly City performance. She gave me my usual Kia-Ora orange cordial drink, and frowned as she gave me a stern look. She twigged within five minutes of my arrival that I was "putting on a face" as she liked to term it, and she knew why. She left me alone that day to stew, because she knew I had to go through the grieving process. Football was how she identified me. When my birthday came around, a City-themed present was always likely, plus a ten pound note inside my card.

I thought she would live forever, despite the weight that hung on her shoulders because outlived her daughter. I am going to miss her so, so much.

I am enlisted to help with clearing the house of my gran. There are a lot of boxes in the loft, all taped up, a chronicle of the past. Some chipped furniture, a lot of paperwork, newspapers and small ornaments, including an old doll that creeps me out. It looks like something from a horror film.

Then I see it. When I was five or six, I decided I was going to make my own birthday card for my gran. My mum was happy to help, though was less content with the glitter I spread round the house. Armed with a Pritt Stick and some left-handed scissors, I got to work. I had chosen City as the theme, because – why not? – and had hand-drawn some players, with one of them saying via a speech bubble, "Man City Say Happy Birthday".

I'm not going to lie, the standard of the artwork was not the best. Most of the players looked like puddles, and I'd struggle to put names to them, so I had written Power (Paul) in tiny letters on the back of one of the shirts. Inside the card, standards improved. My writing is not attractive, something I weakly attribute to being a southpaw. Truth is, I rarely write anymore, I type. I'm out of practice, and impatient when laying down words. But as a child, I had the neatest writing imaginable. I shocked myself when I opened the card.

To Gran,

Hope you have a great day and lots of nice food, and drink too. From me and the players xxx

And she did have a great day, the players less so, who lost, as they often did in those days.

The Season Continues

I was distracted at the next home match, because the futility of it all had been laid bare in front of me that week. For the first time, I felt that none of this mattered. Compared to other stuff going on in life, why did I invest so much in watching others?

I thought it would be good to get out the house, but I was wrong. I could not distract from my misery. City won, so at least there was that, but I returned home in the same state as I had left earlier in the day, a cloud hanging over me.

The funeral was two days later. The turnout was great, which cheered me up. The service was brief, which further improved my mood. Polly did not have many friends left of similar age, but she was still something of a local celebrity, and it was lovely to hear stories from those that knew her.

Perspective

Unfortunately, it takes bad things like this to happen for me to gain some perspective about football. To remember that my football team doing well or doing badly is not the be all and end all. That it is merely a sideshow to more important things, even if it doesn't feel that way most of the time. I'm repeating myself. Anyway, it is often bad things happening within the football stratosphere that jolts me back to reality.

The next "thing" is the ever-constant problem of racism within football, a mirror of wider society. When Liverpool player Luis Suarez receives a hefty ban for racially abusing Manchester United player Patrice Evra, his own manager and teammates wear T-shirts in his support. Tribalism takes over once more, and as sure as night follows day, swathes of Liverpool fans refuse to believe that he has done anything wrong, overnight becoming experts in Uruguayan dialect and slang. What's more, they say, the proof of guilt the FA use is lower than in a criminal court. Perhaps that is worth mentioning, but it is such a delicate issue and there is evidence none of us will have seen, that having an opinion is best left to those in the know. John Terry too has been accused of racially abusing Anton Ferdinand, after QPR beat Chelsea 1-0, and it is Ferdinand and Evra that get booed as they play football. This is the world we live in. Terry is stripped of the England captaincy as investigations begin.

One of my first thoughts is how very different the reaction would have been if this had played out at my football club, and not Liverpool. But that is the wrong reaction, and such whataboutery helps no one.
It would have been different though, for the record.

It is a timely reminder that punishments handed out to players by their own club can be linked to their value as an asset. When Joey Barton stubbed a cigar into the eye of a Manchester City youth player at a drunken Christmas party, it will surprise few to learn that it was the youth player that left the club soon after. Barton has never been the greatest player in the world, but at a time when City courted little success, he was one of the club's biggest assets, and most consistent performers. Which side was the club likely to take? It was never in doubt.

Mr Versatility

Soon after, I had something very different to occupy my mind. One morning I wake up to the news that Gary Speed has tragically taken his own life. He has no connection to my football club, but that is irrelevant. It is heart-breaking to learn that his struggles have defeated him. If anything remotely positive can come of this, then hopefully the news will act as a timely reminder.

If the internet has taught me one thing, it is that it was better in the old days not knowing the thoughts of many of the people around me. Because now I see these thoughts typed out online every day, I worry for the future of humanity. One such thought is the idea that you can't be depressed if you are wealthy and/or successful. It is a staggeringly ignorant view of what depression is, and why it may happen. But ignorance is everywhere. What's more, it seems that some people find it necessary to have an opinion about everything.

I tell a friend all this, about perspective, a few days later. He shrugs his shoulder. You don't need perspective, he argues. It is fine to care deeply about football, and to separate it from the rest of your life and the rest of the world. And yeah, he's right. Sometimes I wish I didn't care so much about football, but that doesn't mean I shouldn't. And it feels like I have little choice, anyway. I'm locked into this.......

The Final Countdown?

.....which is shame, as City lose their crucial Champions League tie to Napoli 2-1, in a fiery atmosphere. A player linked with City in recent times, Edison Cavani, scores twice as Napoli leapfrog the blues in the table. If he is coming to Manchester, I regret it not happening earlier. Napoli have Villareal to play in their final game, so the outlook is bleak, even if City beat Bayern Munich.

The home crowd are on fine form, which is one way to describe it. They are hostile, City players are booed with every touch, and there is an air of menace, as everyone expected. Fireworks are regularly seen flying in all directions, and perhaps this influences the result. It's natural to consider the difference in atmosphere for this game compared to an English game. But how can you compare? I can't take a plastic bottle into the Etihad, so the chances of me slipping in a full pyrotechnic display are slim, at best. If I stand up, someone will complain, and a steward will probably want a word. Perhaps a Latin temperament is required to really get the atmosphere going on nights like this, but in England, there's only so much that can be done. And that so much is singing, and nothing more. We can certainly learn plenty from fan culture elsewhere.

Be Happy For Others

Glass half full, or glass half empty? With the way my life has gone recently, I find myself turning increasingly bitter. This manifests itself in envy at other people's lives.

An example. I log onto Facebook, and my timeline is dominated by photos of beer sat on tables at Manchester Airport. The traditional 6am pint, a rite of passage. Off to Italy, a country I have never visited. A pang of jealousy envelops me, at the thought of my friends embarking on another great trip, that will no doubt provide stories, anecdotes and pleasant memories for many years to come, whatever the result. At least my liver will thank me for staying at home. Perhaps it is bitterness, or perhaps it is a fear of missing out. The jealousy subsides, and I decide I am happy for them. I can't live every experience as a fan, and I don't need to.

Winter Is Coming

City visit Liverpool for the next game, Craig Bellamy given compassionate leave for the home side after the death of his close friend. City draw 1-1, only the second dropped points of the season, so no disaster. The bigger talking point is Mario Balotelli being sent off as a substitute, after picking up two yellow cards in under 20 minutes. Soon after he is scoring a goal against Norwich by allowing the rebound from his saved shot to drop onto his shoulder and into the net. You get a bit of everything with him. I feel his name may crop up again during my musings, hopefully for the right reasons.

A draw at Liverpool is no disaster. I have no idea what is needed to win this league, points-wise, so it's hard to define what pace City must go at. Every season is unique, and the results of title rivals is as important as City's. November is almost at an end, United didn't win either, so City maintain their five-point lead at the top of the table.

December 2011 (almost)

Another day, another competition. This is not like the old days, when reaching the quarter-final of any cup competition made the season feel seminal. City have a tough quarter-final tie at Arsenal in the League Cup, and after being on the back-foot for much of the match, score a brilliant breakaway goal via the twinkle toes of Sergio Aguero with just seven minutes remaining. City are through to another cup semi-final. The win matters to me, but many others will denigrate such progress. The importance of a domestic cup tends to vary according to how well your team performs in it. Get knocked out of the League Cup (or whatever it's called this season), and it's nothing more than a Mickey Mouse Cup. Win it, and it is naturally important silverware. Any silverware is important, certainly right now for my club.

This is all new to me. There was a list that circulated the message boards of City forums for many years of the long succession of teams that had reached a domestic cup semi-final since the last time City did. It essentially lists most of the teams in the country, with Chesterfield standing out for many blues.

This semi-final won't be at Wembley, but will be a two-legged affair against Liverpool, which is not really what City need when challenging for a title over a busy Christmas period. They won't get much sympathy for a fixture pile-up, nor should they.

City have offered hope of cup success before, but always let me down. I'm glad I am just too young to remember the heartache of the 1981 FA Cup final defeat, though if I see that Ricky Villa goal one more time I will smash my TV into a thousand pieces. Ask fans which defeat hit them hardest, and opinions will differ, but the same suspects are usually listed. For me, it was a quarter-final FA Cup defeat at home to West Ham during the bland Stuart Pearce years. There were not many Stuart Pearce years, it just felt like there was. Despite his cautious style of play, I was convinced this was City's year for cup glory. City played Wigan on the Saturday, as I spent a weekend in Whitby with family, feeding endless 10p pieces into amusement arcade relics. City lost, but the match was a mere sideshow before the main event on the Monday night. The key was not to wear out many players considering this strange schedule. Unfortunately, City's big hope up front, Georgios Samaras, got injured, to add to an already considerable list of unavailable players. I was still confident. This was our year.

Or not. Typical City. We played quite well, but didn't take our chances. Had Sun Jihai sent off. Dean Ashton got a brace. City were, once more, out of the FA Cup. And though at some point in every season of my football-supporting season I have had to experience this feeling, twice, it still hurts as much as ever. Will I ever see my team win anything? Will they ever walk out at Wembley? At that moment, the answer felt like an emphatic no. I was out of hope. This is what football can do to you. You enter a ground full of excitement, optimism, confidence. There is a buzz in the air, the atmosphere is electric, and you feel you are about to be part of a special night. Under two hours later, you leave, dejected, shoulders slumped, little more than murmurs in the night air, your dreams smashed to pieces and resigned to your fate.

For other blues, a defeat at Blackburn Rovers hits hardest. Same manager, same stage of the competition, just the following season. Blackburn won 2-0, and even playing with ten men for 20 minutes didn't deter them. Another night that began with such great hope and optimism ended with the away support of 7,000 fans singing, "you're not fit to wear the shirt". Sometimes it's better to know your team is going to be crap, rather than allow them to build up your hopes before destroying them in a flash. And all I could think, as a million fans before me have also thought at some point, was that I deserved better than this. I didn't start supporting this team for glory, but still, come on, couldn't you just once cut me some fucking slack?

It's that time of the year, with the nights drawing in as December arrives, and I am compelled to make the difficult decision of when to switch to my winter coat. Time to take note of temperatures, and perhaps dig out my Maine Road bobble hat, that has served me well down the years. Shorter days affect my wellbeing, and winter is not my favourite time of year, even if there is a smorgasbord (sorry) of football to keep me occupied. By the time we all come out the other side and the clocks spring forward, I will know a lot more about what this season holds. But I find this time of year bleak, the lack of daylight affecting my mood for the worse. I am approaching an age where the winter chill gets into my bones.

But then there is Christmas. Two weeks off work, and a packed social calendar.

Bored in the office, I decide to check on my Fantasy Football team. This is my first visit in months, which explains why there are three injured players in my first XI, and my global position is 2,786,345. Next season, I will definitely take it seriously.

An End And A Beginning

I sit in a cosy pub, as a long column of Bayern Munich fans march past the window chanting in perfect English, the police leading them to the ground with well over an hour to go to kick-off. As always, I expect to get to my seat just in time for the match. Football and choreography combine when there's an overseas team in town.

It's all very impressive, but it's not for me. Freedom to travel and drink where I want, to travel to the ground when I want, and watch the football without being part of a dance troupe.

I've seen the leaders of foreign fans face away from the match for almost 90 minutes as they conduct the choir. I've seen them not even turn round when a goal has been scored. Which makes me wonder what they're doing there in the first place. But hey, I'm English, and getting even more grumpy in middle-age. Visual displays are more my thing, what the Italians may call tifo, though I was once caught under a huge banner being passed along the Kippax and missed the first five minutes of the match.

Admittedly such displays are fascinating to watch, and adds greatly to the atmosphere. And the Premier League and its clubs could do with plenty of guidance on creating an atmosphere, not that the fans themselves are largely to blame. Whatever the rights and wrongs, I would hope that there is one thing we all agree on as we drain our final pint before hailing a taxi to the ground. Drums have no place in a football ground, and anyone caught banging one at a match should receive a lifetime ban, with immediate effect.

My Happy Place

Despite the relatively high stakes, the atmosphere in the pub is good. It's always the same, as if the impending game is not a thing to worry about just yet. Some of my favourite people, taking about nothing of any importance, as a log fire crackles nearby. Sometimes, I never feel more at peace then when relaxing with good friends with a pint of bitter in front of me. I don't need to get drunk, I just need to be there. Someone has come back from the bar with a selection of crisps and some pork scratchings. Can this day get any better? As is often the case, my football team will determine that.

The laugh you have with your friends cannot be surpassed, not even by your favourite comedian. It's the best feeling. A few years ago, a close friend of the group, a fellow match-going blue, died suddenly, aged just 39. The next time we were in the pub for a match, a few weeks later, his absence hung over everyone. We sank some pints and we laughed at jokes, but it all felt forced. It took a few matches before the was some sense of normality. He would never be forgotten, and there would always be a gap in our lives, but eventually, our pub sessions felt like those of old. We had moved on because, well, you have to, don't you? We raised a glass, reminisced, and we carried on.

That's the beauty of a match day, away from the match. People come and go as they please. Everyone just passing through. Some are there as the pub opens, barely functional by kick off. Some pop in for a pint. The hardy few with nothing better to do reconvene post-match. If there is anything to say about the match, good or bad, it is dealt with swiftly. And then back to enjoying a drink with friends, and forgetting any worries, until the morning.

How you experience sport differs for everyone. For me, it has been for a long time about friends. That is who I go with now, not with my dad, or children or any of that. Friends, always. Because of football, I have more friends than I would otherwise have, a lot more. It is not down to my sparkling personality. And because of football, I have spent a lot more time with a core group of friends, and developed stronger relationships as a result. I guess it is what I am used to. If I had gone to the match with my dad all my life, then I would be struggling to let go right now. I'd be considering becoming a non-match attender. But I fell into the communal experience many years ago, and that means that as long as I am fit enough to go to see City, there will be plenty of people to go with me.

Falling Short

Manchester City v Bayern Munich as the final group stage game offered so much potential when the draw was made, but by the time the game arrives, Bayern Munich are through, and a City victory is not enough as Napoli also win their game. It's one of those matches where you're checking other scores as a match progresses, with United also crashing out of the Champions League giving me a slither of contentment. After the chaotic nature of City's early games in the competition, to finish with ten points from six games is no embarrassment, but as Villareal did not pick up a single point, City finish 3rd and are relegated to the Europa League.

This creates a debate in the media about the failure of City to qualify, with their wealth and ambition not mirrored in the campaign. A separate debate develops as to whether it is harder to win the Champions League or the Premier League. For City, the latter always seemed the more likely when the season began, and nothing has changed in that respect. However, debating whether it is harder to win the Premier League or the Champions League somewhat misses the point. Only one team can win either each season, and the likely candidates are usually limited to a select group.

What is more pertinent for me is what winning each of the competitions tells us as fans, and this how we should grade the achievements. They're both great achievements, so fans of the winners should celebrate and waste little time debating which is better. Enjoy the moment. But this is what is key to me. The best team usually wins a league. The best team does not always win a cup competition. So the achievement of winning the Champions League may be every bit as great as winning the Premier League, but the ability to decisively say that team is the best in Europe doesn't wash for me.

Until my team wins it one day, at which point I will of course alter my opinion.

Have Another Go

So, City's European campaign continues. What a ridiculous state of affairs. What sort of set up allows failure to be rewarded this way, by having a crack at the next level down of European competition? It just seems to lay out starkly how UEFA set up competitions not for reasons of fairness, but as a cash cow, often for the status quo, a form of protection when things don't go to plan. It won't be long before certain teams (of which City will never be one) qualify for the Champions League not on merit, but because they used to be good, and threats of a breakaway Super League mean UEFA bows to their demands. Having been starved of European football during my thirty years as a City fan, I do not consider playing in the Europa League as slumming it. But having already played in the Champions League this season, it seems both weird and – well - just plain wrong. I want City to do well, but if we were to win the competition, it would seem a bit hollow.

Favourites

I phone in a local radio station, to discuss my favourite player of all time. Part of me is reticent to do so, because I get a strong feeling that in a few years' time, one of the current squad will be my choice.

So who is your favourite player? Is it the best player at your club, or is there something else that elevates them above everyone else? I think about this as I lie in bed today wracked with guilt at not being up at 10am, wasting the sun's rays that peek through the curtains, worried that I do not make enough use of my waking hours. And when I lie awake in bed, my mind races. This is the latest topic to leap into my head, because I am doubting the choice I made on the radio, Paul Lake, because his career was cut short by injury. Should that matter? I conclude that favourite players earn their status from more than performances alone.

A perfect case in point is Pablo Zabaleta, the sort of player I hope City fans sing about long after he has departed the club. He is a cult hero at City, and I struggle to put into words as to why that is, even if I fully understand why. But I must try.

First off, he is a great footballer. But he is not the greatest. In fact, he is competing with Micah Richards, a lovable youth product, for the right-back spot, so even in his specific position, he has competition for his place in the first XI. But Zabaleta is something special. And when you try to work out why he is held in such high esteem, you form a complete picture of how cult players are created. Firstly, he gets "it". And "it" refers to understanding what is involved in playing for his particular football team, and representing them on and off the pitch. He is a consummate professional, and he is someone who it is clear is not just passing through, does not see football as merely a job, but understands the player/fan relationship, something that has become weakened in recent years as players are increasingly wrapped in cotton wool and exist within their own bubble, at least at the top level of the game. No more getting the bus to the match for these pampered millionaires.

Pablo Zabaleta does not come across as a rich footballer, but an everyday man. He is normal, and approachable, and kind, and gentle. I make him sound like a perfect partner, but he appears to be the most decent man imaginable. And above all, he has embedded himself into Manchester life and into Manchester City Football Club. There are rumours he gets a chippy tea every week, he lives in a modest property and avoids flashy cars. I know nothing of his private life, and have no desire to. He was born half way across the world, and yet more than virtually any other footballer, he feels like one of us. Someone who you would share a pint with, have a laugh, put the world to rights.

And that's why there's a saying amongst some City fans: always try and be yourself, but if you can't be yourself, then be Pablo Zabaleta.
Amen to that.

For some, a favourite will also be considered a cult hero. Often, cult heroes don't even have to be that good at football. Loyalty, effort and personality can be enough. Perhaps one important goal or action on a pitch can lead to immortality.

And then there's Sergio Aguero. He may be too damn good at football to be a cult hero, but he may well become my favourite player. And again, it's not just about the football. Don't get me wrong, the football is amazing. I knew City had signed the real deal, but I had no idea he was this good. That goal at Arsenal was a timely reminder. But surely there has to be more to be a favourite. Because he is surrounded by brilliant players, after all. And with Sergio Aguero, he just has something special, something that is undefinable. He plays with a smile too, and with a degree of innocence. He is the type of player even rival fans would struggle to hate. What's more, he is a forward, and football fans always have a soft spot for a top-class striker. It is said that Newcastle fans, above all, love a "Number 9", but we all do really. And I am beginning to really love Sergio Aguero.

My mind wanders off on a tangent. Are football skills genetic? Many footballers produce offspring that also excel at football. But why is that? Perhaps having a footballer as a parent provides the perfect environment to succeed. If it is genetic, then Sergio Aguero's children should make it right to the top. Sergio is married to the daughter of Diego Maradona, who I assume you know. Therefore, any children the couple have will surely rule the world at some point soon after 2030.

Magic Of The Cup

It's time for the FA Cup 3rd round draw. I love it. A chance to visit a new ground perhaps, if I stand any chance of getting a ticket. I always get a buzz from a cup draw, and the 3rd round of the FA Cup is the king of draws. Yes, there's that pre-draw process once more, but the draw itself is always an adrenalin rush, you just have to nail the time you think the draw itself starts, and hope you're not late. The permutations and the opportunities. And for some fans with any cup draw, the realisation of another adventure on the horizon, be it to Cardiff or Berlin or Doncaster. If it's got an airport or a train station plus a pub, it will do.

The ideal draw is an away tie against a lower-league team – and the lower the better. It is logical to want the easiest ties possible if you wish to win a competition, as this makes winning it more likely. The idea that you must "beat the best sides" to win a tournament is fantasy, as you do not. You can get away with meeting just one if the ties go your way. In 2004, Championship side Millwall reached the FA Cup final, where they predictably were well beaten by Manchester United. I watched the game in a bar in Barcelona with a United-supporting friend, pretending to be pleased with his team's success. The "best sides" Millwall had to conquer to get that far were Walsall, Telford United, Burnley, Tranmere Rovers and Sunderland. Not a single Premier League team amongst them.

Now being drawn at home is even more advantageous, but there is the consideration that it can be quite boring drawing a League 2 side at home, and it will dent my bank balance even more. I am guaranteed to go to a home game, but this is just another way to wear me down because there is just too much football. Many think it is an honour to get to watch your side every week, and I guess it is, but when you get a run of five home games in just a few weeks, it can actually feel like a bit of a drag. I may say more about that when I am feeling more erudite. But ultimately, you want a team outside the Premier League to make progression more likely, and so that the manager is not stretching the squad by being obliged to play his strongest side. An "easy" draw is a great opportunity to see some youth players strut their stuff.

So here we go. It is Sunday afternoon, and Gianfranco Zola, the only opposition player I have ever applauded off a pitch, is helping draw the balls. There are two definite non-league teams in the 3rd round, with four more a possibility, and a trip to Wrexham sounds good to me. I know City's ball number, and have semi-memorised the numbers of the key teams I wish to avoid.

Manchester City are drawn out the hat third, so little tension this time around as the options dwindle, and they will be at home to……….

Manchester United.

I stare at the screen for almost a minute, calmly turn the TV off, and go for a lie down.

I have no choice but to accept two derbies each season. This is the consequence of being competent and a different proposition to the yo-yo club I used to support. But the elephant in the room is that you may meet in various cup competitions, the likelihood of which increases the better the two teams are. Recently, the two Manchester teams were pitted against each other in a two-legged semi-final of the League Cup. Four days of absolute hell in one season, thank you footballing gods. Extra reason for me to embrace atheism, as no deity would punish me in this way. What did I do in a previous life?

Tiring At The Top

All this football is tiring, but the periods in between the matches are worse. Modern life is tiring too. Many of us struggle to sleep, especially those of you with young children. Life is stressful, frantic, tough. Football has always been a release for millions of us. An escape from the grind of daily life. A chance to vent some frustrations, cheer, shout, celebrate. But for many City fans in recent years, it has been anything but an escape. The opposite in fact – it's actually been the most tiring part of our lives. Because for many of us, we have been accused of being little more than trolls, and defenders of human rights abusers. How has it come to this?

I used to go to the football, come home, read a match report then get on with my life – until the next match. If City had lost, and they had a tendency to do just that, I'd have a bit of a sulk, then move on. But then everything changed. The internet became a thing, social media arrived, and everything had to be analysed. Battle lines were drawn, the age of banter dawned, and decent discourse pretty much fizzled away. Having found Twitter quite entertaining when I joined, I am beginning to see its other side now. It's actually common nowadays when City have won a game that I actively try to avoid social media because it will kill my mood. Have I watched the same game as everyone else?

The irony here is that effectively all of this is nothing to do with me. Who owns City, who they buy, the actions of managers, players, the board. Not me, nor you, nor you. The thing is, and you're probably aware of this, is that fans are not responsible for pretty much everything that happens at their football club. We're not running the club. We're not rearranging sponsorship deals or moving money about. We're not scouting Jo. We're not hitting the ball in from thirty yards either. My contribution has been financial, but that doesn't amount to a hill of beans in this money-soaked crazy world of modern football. I've spent thousands on

City, and it would barely cover the weekly expenses for a youth player. But that is to misunderstand fandom of course. We feel responsible. We feel the need to defend our club. We feel what they do rubs off on us, good and bad. They represent us, in a way, we represent them. It thus helps when they don't fuck up.

This is not on us, nothing is. We're allowed as football fans to just go and watch football. Fandom will inevitably lead to some defending the indefensible. For a small section of any club's fan base, their club can do no wrong. The club could put up season ticket prices by 30%, and they would still have their defenders. But beyond that, there is so much drivel, so many mistruths spread, that it is a full-time job just to read it all. The sensible thing of course is to walk away and get on with our lives. Who cares if Dave from Aldershot thinks any success for City is tainted?

When City were taken over in 2008, just a few years ago, life was different. Many of us had internet access naturally, but social media was still in its infancy. Away from message boards, many of which were inhabited by fans of a single club, there was little discourse online about clubs, and much less about owners. I do not have an eidetic memory, far from it, but I don't recall much of an outcry over the new owner, Sheikh Mansour, and his purchase via his investment group (ADUG). Many rival fans, of the clubs that competed for the major honours, initiated a defence mechanism that involved them stating repeatedly that money does noy buy success. Now that City have a cup in their barren trophy cabinet and seem to be Premier League contenders. Suddenly everyone is an expert in human rights, Middle East geopolitics and they are all concerned about the moral aspect of City's ownership model.

Down in London, Roman Abramovich has overseen a period of huge success at Chelsea, and perhaps my memory fails me once more. Because I do not recall the outcry over the source of his funds, and certainly not an incessant undermining of any Chelsea's achievements because of their expenditure and the moral aspect of a Vladimir Putin ally using his questionable funds to bankroll a football team. Maybe I missed the memo.

I think there's a desire to hold football to higher moral ideals, when the truth is it's always had little more than a fleeting relationship with any level of purity. Nowadays, at the top level, it is a playground for billionaires whose sole priorities are becoming even richer and gaining more power. It has many parallels with politics. At a lower level, the sport is blighted by businessmen who say all the right things before asset stripping the club they control, putting its very existence in doubt. All these people, at whatever level they operate at, are considered "fit and proper" by the game's governors and administrators.

Can you be proud of something you have no say over? Or are we all in it to share in other people's glory? I once told a friend, and I don't know why, that I was proud to be left-handed. He asked why I was proud about something I was born with. It's like being proud of having big feet. I didn't have an answer, but then can we be proud to be English, or a City fan? Yeah, damn right we can. If you're a United fan that hates the Glazers, you are no less likely to be proud of your club. The Glazers are not the club, they simply run it, in the same way City's owner does. They'll move on one day, but we won't.

No Need To Apologise

I must be clear on this, that whilst I will be eternally grateful for what our owner has given us, and the memories and associated glory I have already experienced and hopefully will for many years to come, I have no feeling for him on a personal level, nor those running the club at a lower level. I'll enjoy the ride, thanks, without kissing the backside of a billionaire who views me as a number, if he even knew I existed. I have a right to support my club and enjoy its success, without having to apologise for the owner. Fact is, no one cared about City's owner or Middle East geopolitics until City started being a threat to the big boys and won something.

I'll ask again. Should we care anyway? Does it matter what people within your social media bubble are saying about your football club? Was it better when I supported an underachieving club that everyone felt sorry for? Or is it preferable to be hated, and to develop a thick skin and man the barricades for the rest of your lives? I don't have the answers, I just know that as I sigh repeatedly whilst typing these words, I feel tired once more. Oh for the old days when we just talked about the football. That's all I ask for in the future. Before that elusive day though, things are only going to get worse.

Walk away, enjoy life, and you may just sleep sounder because of it. This is not my fight to have.

Mourning Blues

Stop all the clocks, cut off the telephone,
Prevent the dog from barking with a juicy bone,
Silence the pianos and with muffled drum,
Bring out the coffin, let the mourners come.

Manchester City have lost a football league match, and I am down, the dodgiest of penalty decisions ensuring Chelsea win the game 2-1. City are still top by two points.

I miss the game as I am off to see a comedian at the Lowry theatre in Salford Quays. It will feel weird not seeing my team play live. It's been over a year since this is the case. And in a world where being a supporter can seem like a competition sometimes, where you must prove how big a fan you are, there is a sense of guilt at skipping a match to do something else instead. In fact right now on Twitter, there is a dreary argument between match-going fans and those that live far away from their team's ground about what constitutes a "proper" fan. Getting up at 4am to watch City is a commitment every big as going to games, many claim. What seems weird to me is that you can't even be a casual fan anymore online, it has to be all or nothing.

The real issue with not watching the match live is that I am on edge, not knowing what is going on, relying on staggered online information no the BBC site, and my Twitter timeline that seems to struggle with impartiality. So until the match is over, there is no chance of relaxing.

The Joy Of Football

There's a man on the tram shouting into his phone to an unknown person, presumably a City supporter, that his team will never match the experiences he has had as a fan of a traditional big club.

I was once mocked by a fan of a "big" and successful club for stating that the season in the Championship under Kevin Keegan was one of my greatest experiences as a fan. People like him don't understand the real world. They think that enjoyment can only be experienced by being the best in the world, lording it over rival fan bases, getting right to the top of the tree. If your greatest memories do not include all of that, then you are "small-time", to directly quote him. Getting enjoyment from being a football supporter is unique to every one of us. A Rochdale fan is as entitled to experience happiness in Division 2 as a Barcelona fan is. It's about experiences, forging memories, unexpected victories, and your team ultimately putting a smile on your face. Nothing makes me roll my eyes more than hearing a fan proclaim that their club is back where they belong, as if they have a greater entitlement to success. A club belongs where its football takes it. One season of watching Ali Bernarbia strut his stuff is equal to any trophy. It's all relative to expectation.

Winter Blues

On 18th December, City beat Arsenal 1-0 and return to the top of the table. That is what the BBC report says anyway, giving me something else to get annoyed with. City started the day top, but United won earlier in the day, so nothing has really changed. Surely teams can only return to the top if the team previously top drops points? This was a nervy game. Recently I have noticed a few grey hairs showing through, and I wonder how many more will now surface this season, and not just after this game, one that City shade with a David Silva goal. This is one of the many games where the result is everything, as it comes after a defeat, so there is a need for redemption. They, whoever they are, used to say a result like this was the form of champions – winning when not at your best. I just see it as worrisome that form may dip going into a crucial part of the season. Never satisfied.

It's a cold day, bitterly so, to the extent that I only spot three men in my part of the ground wearing shorts. There's always a small section of the fanbase allergic to trousers. I have miscalculated the journey to the ground as I am not in the pub pre-match, due to a heavy Christmas works do the night before. I drink too much tequila and am sick by 6pm, before rallying during the evening. Drink is the only way to deal with some of my colleagues in social situations.

I am thus in my seat too early. I get thinking of the coldest I have ever been in a football ground, as there is no one to talk to for ten minutes. There is no competition for me, as I think back to the time me and a friend had a spare Saturday, so decided to take in Bolton Wanderers v Tranmere Rovers at Burnden Park. We were at the end opposite the supermarket that resided in one corner, and I do not recall anything of interest happening on the pitch, though Bolton may have scored a scrappy goal at some point. I will not forget thinking I had frostbite across the lower half of my body. Then there was a Europa League game at home to PSG. Manchester was gridlocked by frost and ice and I was one of the few who made it to the ground, which allowed me to spread my legs. As is traditional, there was precious little football to grab my attention, and the away fans fought amongst themselves at one point in a desperate attempt to stay warm. Then there was a match at home to Southampton on New Years' Day. Badly hungover, I decided to get a bus to the ground from West Didsbury, and for reasons I cannot fathom, I left the house on a rainy, cold, January day wearing just a flimsy summer jacket. The bus never arrived, but a fellow blue at the stop shared a taxi to the ground. Heavy traffic prevented it getting close to the ground, so I walked the final mile in torrential rain, and spent the match worrying those sat around me that I may have contracted hypothermia. I had to be fed Bovril to keep my head above water.

Love It!

It's the fabled Christmas schedule. Fans love it, so we are constantly told. Managers certainly don't. But hey, tradition and all that. You can't mess with it, though those in power have, as teams used to play on Christmas Day. Ultimately, this brutal period favours the bigger teams, as most things do. Despite what people may say, their squads are not bigger, but they are better, and importantly, deeper. It's a lot easier to rotate your squad when you've got eight seasoned internationals ready to step in.

As for me, I am not totally on board with games every few days, as it just adds to the stress. But it depends who the opposition teams are, and how the games fall. A home game on Boxing Day is often a delight, at least half the crowd clearly ecstatic at getting away from the family. A home game on New Years' Day is the worst news imaginable, as I will inevitably have a hangover to nurse. Thankfully this season City are away on 1st January, so that won't be an issue this time around.

Christmas Cheer

Christmas Day is spent the same way as always. I am in charge of the gravy, and as always I nail it - you could stand a spoon up in it. It's heartburn central, straight to the hips and worth every mouthful.

I am an atheist, but the day has never been about religion anyway, at least in my family, much of which consists of in-laws nowadays. A chance to get together, eat too much and watch mediocre TV shows. An annual reminder that Doctor Who is awful, and what's with that cringey background music?!

There is carnage as presents are exchanged. I never get anything football-related as an adult, probably because it is assumed I already own anything City-related that I want, especially book-wise. But these moments are nice, a rare part of the year when gifts are exchanged both ways. My dad is both here, and absent, if you know what I mean.

On Boxing Day, I devour some leftover cheese and crackers, before watching a dull 0-0 draw against West Bromwich Albion, the first time City have failed to score all season. They are hanging on to top spot on goal difference, and my nerves continue to jangle. I may have five more months of this, and the strain is showing. I wonder if it ever gets any easier? Are these beginner's nerves?

Getting Away

Away days requires leaders and followers, because it requires schedules and organisation. I am a follower, who is happy to go with the flow and follow the itinerary set by others. Some people are just better at organising group trips, mostly because they enjoy doing so. I buckle under the responsibility.

The leaders in the group live for days like this. Anything in London, and/or any trip where an overnight stay is on the cards, well that's the jackpot. The time of the train, what to drink on the journey, where to drink once the destination is reached, post-match locations, the train back and more. Like planning a holiday, it is fun to map out the day, with military precision. Wembley visits are the best, as the whole capital is a potential playground, and the options are endless.

Perhaps with further success, City fans will become dab hands at such organisation. Already, with one Wembley visit, there are ideas for how to work the system in the future, as we must, because following a football fan near and far is an expensive business, and becomes more expensive the more success they attain.

In our group, we all have different ideas of what and where makes for a perfect away day. London will always feel like an adventure, even though I've been there a hundred times and could never live there. Its opportunities for a day out are limitless. I guess to answer what makes for perfection is impossible, but to even attempt to, I must separate English trips from foreign jaunts.

A two-hour train journey is long enough. The journey back can feel double the length after a loss. A new ground is a bonus, good pubs, and a good away allocation.

Some trips gain notoriety and provide fond memories only long after the event, as at the time no one was laughing or having much fun. A cancelled flight in Milan due to snow meaning a night sleeping on an airport floor. The hotel room with mould, one bed for three people and a shower that only deposited ice-cold water. The Danish bar full of bikers who seemed likely to kill us at any moment. Train cancellations, diversions, bad weather, fights in the away end, hostile locals and more. Trips do not always go smoothly. But as long as no one died, in time you see the funny side of it all.

As for the perfect schedule, it has changed little down the years. In England, an unhealthy breakfast followed by an early train. A table seat is preferable. Cans for the journey, snacks too. Many hours before kick-off, it is imperative to be settled in a pub. Usually, more than one pub should be visited before the match itself. A taxi to the ground, ideally getting to your seat just minutes before the match starts. A resounding win, applaud the players off, back into the town centre, a couple hours more pub time, train home with more cans, then a taxi ride no one will remember the next day. Travelling abroad is a very different experience. Probably best to go somewhere that you would not otherwise go.

There is something so special about a domestic away day though. It feels like a mini-holiday, but without having to go through security. If football is a form of escapism for some fans, from the stresses of life, then it is logical that away trips, because they involve travelling further away from home, increase that sense of escapism.

Planning

"What time's the train to Birmingham?"
"8:45."
"Isn't that a bit early?"
"Nah, arrive by 10:30, Spoons will be open."
"How many cans you taking for journey?"
"Four each I reckon."
"I'll book the cab for 8:00 then?"
"Make it 7:45. Gives us time to go to Greggs and get a bacon butty. And nab a table on the train if they cancel reservations."
"OK. Got to swing round Chorlton and pick up Tommy too."
"Bring the cards. In case we get bored."
"Graham's coming, so I'd say that's guaranteed."

Another Year Ends

New Year's Eve is perfect, in that I spend it at someone's house, and not out and about. I have some bad memories of this night from my youth, so it is not my favourite time of the year. Clubs charging £20 to get in, drinks at double their normal price, then a five mile walk home because the chances of hailing a taxi are less than a trouble-free night spent with Mario Balotelli, a crate of fireworks and a lighter. But as a football fan, there are other things to consider, namely when the next game is. My hangovers are brutal, and always have been, so the next day has to be planned for. Or simply endured.

It is Sunderland that City travel to the following day, so I do not need to drag myself to the match whilst trying not to be sick. Or so I thought. Two of my friends are going to the North East the next day, and they seem to be able to shake off hangovers in minutes, so are drinking freely. And they have a surprise for me - they have bought me a present, which is unexpected, as we don't do presents. I open a plain envelope, to discover a train and match ticket for the following day. My face must have been some sight when I released what they had got me, a face of contrasts. The pleasure at such a wonderful gesture, that even a grumpy ageing man like me could get emotional about. However, the immediate thought was the clear understanding that I would have to get up very early indeed the next day, with a hangover. This was both brilliant and terrible news at the same time.

2012

The alarm goes off. With a quarter of one eye open, I note it is indeed 6:30 am as expected. I have allowed five minutes in the schedule to compose myself, but quickly realise that I require five hours. A cursory shower does not improve my wellbeing, and soon I am in a taxi having forced one slice of toast down. Nausea is a constant companion. A coffee at Piccadilly Station improves my consciousness marginally. I know that at some point during the day, the excesses of the previous day will be wiped away and suddenly I will feel normal again, if perhaps a tad tired. But I never know when this moment will arrive, and the only certainty is that it is some way away.

I do my heavy breathing exercises on the long journey to Newcastle (there is no direct train to Sunderland). There are plenty of blues on the train, and the beer is flowing elsewhere. The smell knocks me sick. A quick pint in Newcastle is not possible for me, and I leave most of it. An hour later, I feel some sense of normality, and am back drinking.

On to the ground. The game is a battle, City hit the bar, and then, with a drab 0-0 draw on the cards, a disappointing result in itself, deep into injury time Sunderland score a winner despite their player being yards offside. The linesman is half asleep and City have lost. My friends stand up and depart the stadium the second the ball hits the back of the net. All that way, for this. This is how it is. More drinks, shake off the result and try to have a good time. There's another game next week. Back home, for sleep and abstinence.

It is easy to look at this day and write it off as a disaster. But while I am hugely disappointed by the result, it is nothing of the sort, as many football fans will surely understand. Away days must be cherished even if the match itself lets you down. After all, they are about more than the result. It's about the craic, the travel, the shared experiences, the scrapes, the memories. It's still good to win the game too, don't get me wrong. But for a mid-season league game, the result isn't everything. A trip to Wembley, well that's a slightly different matter.

Logic Departs

The logic of football fans always amuses me, in as much as we are devoid of it when it suits us. Because while almost every single football fan on the planet considers themselves 100% impartial, every single football fan is wrong. We're biased, prejudiced and see what we want to see.

We lack logic in other ways too. Part of the appeal of football, like any sport, is its unpredictability. Without it, it would be very boring, and yet this week I read fans on a message board incredulous that City can score six goals at Old Trafford, but not score against West Bromwich Albion. Or scratch their heads at Sunderland beating Manchester City, then losing to a far inferior side. Is it really that baffling? And despite my current mood after a damaging week, would we really have it any other way?

When Worlds Collide

January means the African Cup of Nations, and Yaya Tore's absence is hitting City, proving just how important he is to the team, even in such a well-stacked squad. The player much of the media thought was overpriced when he moved to City, and was little more than a defensive midfielder, knowledge gained from watching a single Champions League match.

Every time this tournament comes around, there is a predictable reaction from a vocal minority, namely that tournaments should not be played in the middle of a season. It's a naïve and ignorant viewpoint, but one to be expected from those that live in their little protected Western bubble. Climate is obviously a factor here, and it must be acknowledged that not every league starts in August and runs until May. This is a huge tournament for the continent, and for all involved. Perhaps the real issue is that it does not get the respect it deserves. This disrespect shows itself in the many suggestions that I see from fans that players should refuse to go, and remember instead who pays their wages. Imagine suggesting a player should not represent their country at the Euros. That of course would never happen, irrespective of what time of the year it was held. It is unfortunate that the tournament is every two years, ramping up the dissent, but moving the tournament to the summer greatly restricts potential hosts due to the climate issues, which involves rain as well as heat. Clubs just have to accept losing a player or three for a month, and get on with it.

Out The FA Cup

The game is one that results in so many mixed emotions I cannot do them justice on these pages. City lose at home to United, and are out of the FA Cup at the first hurdle, so will not be retaining the trophy. This naturally means I am gutted. But the score does not tell the full story, far from it. Vincent Kompany is sent off in the first half for a tackle that no one in the ground even considered a foul, and from that moment on, they were doomed. A foul where Nani, the sort of player who would go down clutching his knee if a fly collided with his leg, did not even claim for anything. One person in the entire stadium saw something, and unfortunately that one person was the referee, Chris Foy. A terrible decision that ruins a huge match. City are behind by this point so maybe would have lost anyway, but now we will never know.

But still by the end, I felt upbeat too. City were three down by half-time and I feared that United were going to inflict a similar defeat as City had at Old Trafford. But no. City rallied, scored twice and by the end the visitors were glad to hear the final whistle despite their man advantage. A match both set of supporters could take something from. Ultimately though, it's the result that matters.

It is beginning to feel like City are cursed in cup competitions. In the League Cup semi-final 1st leg, City are poor, and lose 1-0 to Liverpool. In the 2nd leg, it is much more competitive, but City are undone by another horrendous decision, that may have been key as the game ends in a draw, leaving City one goal short of parity. A shot hits Micah Richards on his foot and bounces up onto his arm, and the referee gives a penalty. Yet again, match officials have taken centre stage, for all the wrong reasons. Wembley will have to wait for another season.

It is logical for a football fan at this point to claim that the world is against their team and that they are not getting decisions, but fans of every team probably think that. You remember the bad decisions, but are quick to gloss over and forget the moments that went your way. Still, now I can pretend that going out the cups is good news, as "we can concentrate on the league". My bank manager is certainly going to be happier at City's failures. He's been leaving messages on my landline for three months now. Nothing to worry about, he says, just looking to have a chat. I'll pass, thanks.

Dad

"It was Leeds United at home."

"What was?"

"Your first ever game. Leeds United at home."

"What, really? Are you sure?"

"Yes, in November 1977, bitterly cold I think. Peter Barnes and Mick Channon scored, but City lost 3-2."

"Wow. Did I enjoy it all?"

"It's hard to say, you slept through most of it."

"Oh."

"Then wet yourself in the car."

"Oh."

"I think you missed mum."

Manchester City 3 Tottenham Hotspur 2 & More.

This is the sort of game that encapsulates football fandom. Games that put you through the wringer. Highs, lows and everything in between. Huge drama, much of it late, before a last-gasp winner, and I am exhausted just from watching it. I leave the ground feeling as if I had been playing for the last half-hour.

It provides more redemption for City, who lost the same fixture two seasons ago to a Peter Crouch goal, which was key to Spurs qualifying for the Champions League instead of City. Last season, Peter Crouch scored in his own net and City finished in the top four come season-end. Now City need the points just as much as in previous seasons, and a single goal separates the teams for the third successive Etihad game. Spurs are launching their own title challenge and are still in the hunt after this defeat, so it could be a vital three points.

To be fair, it was a game that took time to get going, and then it *really* got going. City take the lead in the 56th minute through Samir Nasri. Three minutes later the lead is doubled, Joleon Lescott sliding over the line with the ball. His goal celebration was cruelly cut short by party pooper Vincent Kompany, who held onto him for dear life.
Seven minutes later and it's somehow all square, and late on Jermaine Defoe was centimetres away from grabbing a late winner, before Mario Balotelli was fouled in the area and despatched the penalty to give City all three points. A breathless 2nd half, with the nerves of a late penalty to decide the game. I'm not sure why I was nervous though – Mario Balotelli may have his faults, but he does not miss penalties.

The drama of the 2nd half, and the importance of the game ensures there is a cracking atmosphere in the ground. The celebrations after the winning goal are up there with the best, and I even join in with some singing, until my throat is coarse.

Truth is, I'm not a singer. I've never started a chant in my life. I'm an introvert, and so am the last person to suddenly stand up and encourage those around to join me in song. I'm even self-conscious when singing as part of a crowd. If you heard me in the shower, you'd understand why. I once decided against ordering a sizzler plate in a Chinese restaurant, as I did not want to draw attention to myself. But when I am singing until my throat is dry, you know it's a good match. The win keeps City three points ahead of United, with a far superior goal difference. So they can afford a slip-up and remain top.

And slip up is what they then went and did.

City lose 1-0 to Everton, and I am not remotely surprised. Everton are a bogey team for City. Most teams used to be, but at last the list is dwindling. Actually, can you have bogey teams if you are generally rubbish? City have won the odd home game against Everton, but their Goodison record is poor. The last time I was at Goodison, City lost 2-0. There was a pole in front of my seat so I couldn't see much of one of the penalty areas, but by the end of the match I was quite grateful for the restricted view. Robinho came on as a substitute, and was so bad he was subbed back off, the ultimate ignominy.

The only entertainment for away supporters occurs when a fan handcuffs himself to a goal post, delaying the game for five minutes. Apparently, Ryanair had sacked his daughter. A defeat for City always stings, and increases the pressure on the subsequent games. Never mind, City are still top, but only on goal difference. That big win at Old Trafford earlier in the season is proving to be rather handy right now.

To make matters worse, ex-United player Darren Gibson scores the solitary goal, goals for him as rare as a bad hair day for Roberto Mancini. I think all football fans think there is at least one player that only seems to score against them, or a keeper that always has a worldie, before playing terribly the week after. In my head right now, that player is David Batty, goals not being a big part of his game. I look up his stats, and he has scored two of his eight league goals against City. Yeah, I'll take that as proof, near enough.

Fulham, Aston Villa, Blackburn Rovers and Bolton Wanderers. Four games follow that present City with a good chance to consolidate their position at the top of the table, and put this defeat behind them. And they do so, winning all four games without conceding a goal.

Senses

City beat Fulham 3-0, and I'm enjoying the match more than usual, though I am not sure why. I am just in a good mood, and early in the match, I realise City are not going to spoil that mood. Sometimes you know within ten minutes of a game how it will go, and this fits the bill. My mind begins to wander in my relaxed state, and I take in the sensory aspects of being at a match, as I gaze around the ground. The sounds of football thrill me. A ball hitting a post hard. The swell of a crowd. The undefinable noise that comes from a mass of people celebrating a goal. A chant that snowballs in size and volume. Individual advice given to a referee. Boos, cheers, the peep of a whistle. Seats clanking up and down as the bar is now open and the bladder is full. The claps, the chatter, the undulation of it all.

And then there are the smells. The outside toilets at the back of the Kippax still send a shiver down my spine when I look back. Better instead to think of the odours of meat and potato pies, Bovril, stale booze. And for some reason, about 15 minutes into the 2nd half in games this season, the smell of toast briefly wafts past my nostrils.

There are many who love a 5:30pm Saturday kick-off time, which is what the Fulham match is, giving ample time for liquid refreshments prior to the match. 3pm remains the perfect time for me, the traditionalist in me kicking in. The early kick-off time on Saturday has both advantages and disadvantages. You will be watching the game sober, but win the game and you've got the whole weekend to relax and enjoy the result. Lose, and the weekend is ruined. However, playing on a Sunday has never felt truly natural to me, and playing a big game then means it can hang over you on the Saturday, as the nerves increase. Winning a game before rivals have played can have a psychological effect.

Losing will simply spur them on. So ultimately, whether kicking off at a certain time is good or bad depends on the result. I feel like I've gone round in circles here.

For me, there is another consideration to make though. In my head, kick-off times have other consequences, because the kick-off time of a match can affect my confidence in my team getting a result. This is almost certainly an irrational argument, but it resides in my brain nevertheless. If City are playing a team perceived to be weaker, there is no better time to play than 3pm on Saturday, not live on UK TV, so somewhat away from the limelight. A night match is the worst time to play a team whose stadium is fairly small, compact, and thus generates a raucous atmosphere, which is only exacerbated by playing late in the day. Personally, I hate games at 12:30pm on a Saturday as I have a vague hunch that City don't perform at that time, though I have no evidence to back this up.

Mario Balotelli Update

Roll up, roll up, get your latest Mario Balotelli news. Your weekly update on the escapades of Manchester City's lovable rogue. So what is it this time? He is charged and suspended for three league matches and the 2nd leg of the League Cup semi-final for a stamp on Scott Parker during the 3-2 win over Tottenham. Yet again, he does himself no favours. Having said that, the evidence does not show a deliberate stamp, and is not conclusive about his intentions when flicking a foot back towards Parker. An element of doubt doesn't seem to matter unless you are the England captain, City don't appeal, and he is out of action for a while.

Too Much

With the rise of the internet, the print media is struggling. How much football is there to talk about? Every day I see articles that eek of desperation, simply filling space, because every single facet of the game must be explored, debated and argued over until there's nothing left, so we start over again. Internet clicks are the future, not newspapers sold. Getting someone to click on a webpage is a very different process and skill to getting someone to buy a newspaper. But what appears online is not always that different from what appears in print.

I am a man of routine, and Wednesday is sandwich day. There is a selection of newspapers to peruse whilst I wait for my club special to be made. I pick up one, and go straight to the back pages, naturally. It is Arsenal v Spurs in a couple of days, and there is a two-page spread debating a mixed XI. I hate them. The ex-Spurs player naturally favours a team made up mostly of Spurs players. The ex-Arsenal player favours a team made up mostly of Arsenal players. What a surprise, and what a waste of everyone's time.

In another paper, there is an opinion piece about how this Arsenal side compares with The Invincibles, and others from the past. Truth is, a top team in 2012 would run rings around any team from 20+ years ago. The Brazil team of 1970 would be chasing shadows. OK, I can never prove that of course, but I think my point is that even if this is demonstrably true, it doesn't mean that the teams of today can be considered "better", because you cannot compare teams across generations. Teams evolve, humans do, and once upon a time sport science became a thing. Technology advances and science always does, and today's athletes live in a different world to those of just twenty years ago. It is impossible to compare the merits of Puskas against Ibrahimovic. And I am not sure why anyone would want to anyway.

If I open the sports pages of a newspaper, what do I want to see there instead? It's hard to say, because all the information I need on my club is available at the click of a mouse. Match reports when I watch every game become pointless. Opinion pieces often tell me what I already know. Perhaps I am in the minority in wanting something more grown-up in the coverage of my side. Maybe newspapers and football websites are giving people what they want. On Facebook, I see the proliferation of football "banter" pages, and thousands upon thousands of people posting juvenile gibberish, day after day. Perhaps I have got this all wrong. Perhaps this is the level of football interaction most fans live for. A race to the bottom, in an attempt to proclaim your team is top.

The Forgotten Games

I don't have a great memory. That's why I don't remember that much about childhood, apart from it being very pleasant and normal. I can't recall every moment like some people can. There was plenty of French cricket, Juicy Lucy lollies and those bubble-gum balls at the bottom of the ice cream. Wembley in Heaton Park when they decided to keep the posts up off-season. Cycling up that really tough hill and the ride in the ambulance when my mate decided to go no-handed over some speed bumps. Grounded for HIS fuck up. Much more snow in those days, building igloos using shopping bags. My progression of bikes, the scrapes that resulted, kicking a football against a wall for hours at a time during summer boredom, being called home from my friend's back garden to hear my grandad had died and being too young to know how to act. Holidays in England. Blackpool illuminations, Scarborough and its funicular, the trek down to Devon and summers in Torquay and the model village in Babbacombe. My fold away snooker table, box rooms and Superman wallpaper. And that huge rhododendron in the back garden that ate footballs for fun.

But nowadays, my memory is terrible. I do not remember basic things, such as what I had for my tea yesterday, ordering the package that had just been delivered (was I drunk at the time?) and when discussing football, the years when certain events happened, and even more so, the years City players were at the club. Ask me when Sylvain Distin signed for Manchester City, and I could easily be five years out. But certain things break through, with astonishing clarity, as they do for my dad occasionally. I remember the worst burger I ever tasted outside Villa Park, before a young Micah Richards scored a last-gasp equaliser in the FA Cup, before gaining infamy by swearing in the post-match interview. I remember getting back in the car afterwards, and drinking a specific beer on the journey home. I remember being refused entry to a pub after a home game against Everton because I had a City training top on under my coat, and I remember exactly the face of the bouncer and the Tim Cahill header that had already annoyed me that day. And yet there are games I know I must have been at, that I have zero recollection of, even when I see the highlights. Maybe that is linked to the standard of the opposition or the importance of the match, but there is still a degree of randomness in my football memory. I think about this as I leave the ground after a 2-0 win over Bolton Wanderers. I guarantee that if you ask me about this match in five years' time, I will refuse to accept it ever happened, or that David Pizzaro started for City. Mario Balotelli scores, and City are five points clear at the top. This is City's 19th successive home win in the league, and the ground is half-empty as the final whistle goes, victory so assured that many have long-gone.

I remember the dates of many events in my life solely because of the football matches that occurred at similar times. Weddings on the same day that Shaun Goater scored that crucial goal against Wigan. My first day working at Argos that was followed by a night game against Sheffield Wednesday.

Football can be an amazing way to recall your past. Ask me what I was doing when Shaun Wright-Phillips was sold to Chelsea for £21m, and I can tell you everything about that moment, and the day that followed. I was at my friend's parents' villa in Portugal. I was alone, as everyone else had headed off to the local village to do a big shop. Despite the knowledge that nowhere outside the UK can make nice crisps, I had requested a few packets, and a water melon. I was sat inside, in the conservatory, taking shelter from the midday sun. There was a beach ball in the pool. That evening, we would all dine at a local restaurant, and I would eat prawns and peri peri chicken. I remember it all vividly.
I remember it all because of the text I received. City had sold their

best player. I knew it was coming. But still, it hurt, and it was now official. I wondered if shedding a tear was appropriate for such an occasion. All I knew was that the day was ruined, and perhaps the next one too. At 11am, I raised a glass.

A Monent Of Clarity

I get the tram home by myself. The carriages are full, fuelling my claustrophobia. I find a seat though, and feel better. I feel serene too. There is blue everywhere, and I experience a wave of contentment, as if I have been transported into the midst of a sickly sweet Christmas movie. I swear every time I make this journey, it seems longer than the previous time, but on this occasion, I don't mind.

Two elderly men sit with their canes, discussing the majestic David Silva. A father and son are reading the match programme together. There's a young girl clutching a City flag as if her life depends on it. Three young lads look bored, and a young woman provides a full match report to someone on the other end of a phone line. Slowly the tram becomes less busy with each stop, as everyone walks off into the night, happy once more because of their football club.

Freedom

"How was Spain?"

"Nice, good to relax, quite warm too for the time of year."

"You didn't miss much. Though I had to walk back into town by myself after the Bolton match. It annoys me when people leave early."

"Why? They've bought a ticket, they can do what they want."

"Yeah, but it looks shit."

"To who? The club make it impossible to get away from the ground quickly, people have other commitments sometimes."

"To the players. Imagine the full-time whistle going after a good win and the stands are half empty."

"That's the problem of the collective. Individual people have a right to leave when they want, but if loads do it, then it's not a great look. But as I said, don't worry about it. They're not going to hand in transfer requests out of disgust."

"If a league was on the line, they'd manage to stay to the end."

"Yeah but most weeks it isn't, so that's irrelevant."

"Well, it just winds me up."

"You go to the bar 10 minutes before half time some weeks."

"That's different. I haven't left the ground have I? You can't get served otherwise."

"Seat's still empty though. Just let people do what they want."

"You wouldn't leave the cinema ten minutes before the end of a film."

"That's hardly the same is it? Unless you know how the film ends. If City are three up, there's no plot points to come."

"I just don't get it, sorry."

"I can see that. Did you get the pork scratchings?"

"Ah sorry, forgot."

The Family

I met many of my football family online. I lurked on a message board for two years, I then tentatively began to post my own opinion here and there. It would be three more years before I took the next step, a leap of faith, by meeting some of the board members face-to-face.

I have a set of friends brought together by a shared passion. I can meet any one of them, buy a pint and sit there chatting for as long as we desire. And that's how I end up where I am today. A guy I first experienced by seeing his posts under the user name "Kinky7", a reference to Georgi Kinkladze, not his sexual preferences. This faceless poster spoke a lot of common sense, and possessed the gallows humour necessary to support our club. Turns out he was called Frank, and he lives three streets away. Today I sit in a pub, three days after his father has died.

He walks into the pub a few minutes after me, and we hug. I buy him a pint and a packet of Quavers. I pat him on the shoulder, offer my condolences, and we raise our glasses. I sense he does not want to talk about what has happened, he just wants to talk about unimportant stuff and get drunk, so that is what we do. I wouldn't know what to say anyway. I tear open the packet of crisps for easy access, and for a short while once more, we forget about the rest of the world.

Jack Of All Trades

Being a football supporter used to be about, funnily enough, watching football. Not anymore. Nowadays, as a City fan, I am expected to be an expert in finance, human rights issues in the Middle East, and before that, Thailand. I feel compelled to have a robust opinion on market values of footballers, player amortisation, Financial Fair play rules, TV rights, ticket prices, and much more. I'm happy to have these opinions, most of the time, but I do miss the old days when ignorance was bliss. When the only thing that mattered was how well the team played. When my main concern was contemplating whether City would ever win an away game again (they went a whole season without doing so).

I'm only now getting my head round tactics. In the past you could rely on a 4-4-2 formation and lumping it up to the big lad for knock-downs. Now it's la pausa, half-spaces, inverted full backs, overloads, false 9s, zonal marking and more. It's fun to learn, but it feels more like a full-time job to be a fan if you decide to throw yourself into it like many have.

Back In The Pub

I sit in the pub and ask for help over a pint or five. I need to write a fanzine article the next day, and have decided on the topic: why is football so popular? Problem is, I have no idea, but I am determined that this is the article I will submit. So I ask my friends, and they are not much help either. Shrugged shoulders, and one reply of – it just is. I can't stretch that out to a thousand words.

Perhaps the answer lies in working out why many other things in the world are so popular. Is Coca Cola the nicest drink you've ever tasted? That is subjective of course, in the same way that declaring what the greatest sport is. That fizzy beverage was marketed so well it became ubiquitous, and once it was, its success was self-fulfilling. Football was spread round the world by a small number of (mostly) English travellers, and that helped it spread around the globe, at the time of a British Empire, when lots of things, good and bad, were spread around the world. So maybe it's that simple, though it doesn't explain how it spread around Europe. All sports are great, but ultimately one took hold more than any other. Or, as my friend Steve remarked, perhaps it's just because you can pick up a football and play anywhere. Anyone can play football. It is cheap to do so. Its action is near-continuous, and the length of a match fits well with a human's concentration span, or it used to. Underdogs can succeed, which leads to unpredictability. The growth of fierce rivalries and the popularity of flagship tournaments at club and international level have ensured its constant growth. Ultimately, it's more fun watching people kick a ball rather than throw it.

Bumps In The Road

I lost a bit of my passion for football whilst at university as I spent what money I had on beer and fried chicken. I rarely went to matches for a few years, but my distraction from the first love of my life was never going to be permanent, just a natural consequence of living independently for the first time ever, but on a student loan. I was 100 miles away from Manchester most weekends, enough distance to make going to home games more difficult. I had no one to go with either, no support network. My dad had a new job with British Rail, and his hours were all over the place. The season ticket had been abandoned, and he went alone to occasional matches when he had the energy. He said he enjoyed the solitude of attending alone, ignoring the small matter of the 30,000 or so people sat or stood around him. In January 1994 we went to Maine Road together to watch City play Arsenal. It finished 0-0, and I didn't rush to suggest a return visit. It would be 18 months until we went together again. Something was missing, and I couldn't work out if it was to do with football, or the relationship I had with my dad. And I didn't want to know. As far as my dad was concerned, he just slowly lost the enthusiasm to go to matches. For me, I would be back, not just because after university I regained the desire to go back, but also because I got my first credit card, starting me along the path of a lifetime of debt. As always my timing was impeccable, coinciding with the lowest ebb in City's history.

Compromise

There's Just two of us in the pub for now. Ste is talking.

"I told Marie three weeks into our relationship that football was a vital part of my life. I knew then that this was serious between us both, so I had to make it clear. I wasn't going to change. I go to matches, I have some drinks, if City are playing, you won't see much of me that day, until I stagger in around 10pm, often with a Chinese takeaway. It was difficult at first, because Saturday night was seen as the social night of the week, and I was expected to do things as a couple. But often City were playing that day. Sometimes I was hundreds of miles away. Her friend network had to take up the slack. But this is my thing, it's what I do. My passion. I wasn't laying down the law, declaring who wore the trousers in the relationship. I just had to keep this part of my life. Anyway, the longer we were together, the less friction it caused. Nowadays, she can't wait to get rid of me. Means I'm not hogging the TV with the Racing Channel on for five hours."

I don't recall why we are having this discussion. It may be linked to a moment of weakness, when I looked at Claire's Facebook page, and noticed plenty of photos of her and a man I do not recognise. This was inevitable, but it knocks me back for most of the day. Football and the pub becomes my refuge once more.

It's What We Do

It is about compliance. It's an important word when discussing English football, at least at the top level. There is a reason that average season tickets in the Premier League have gone up over 1000% since it began and the grounds are fuller than ever. There's a reason too that there is a tacit acceptance of the product that the Premier League provides for us. That we are swayed by the bling and the brand. It's because English football fans are some of the most compliant, passive and gullible in the world. We are avid match goers and whatever we have to endure, we keep going. Over land, over sea. That's not a negative of course, but it does have the consequence of many of us putting up with whatever is thrown our way. Matches are played at all hours, often with no public transport back afterwards. Games are moved at short notice, then moved again, fans pay thousands of pounds for a season ticket. We pay £100 plus each month for the privilege of watching matches at home. At the ground, we pay five pounds for cooking lager, three pounds for a Bovril or a Kit Kat. And we keep going, due to our love of the game. No other country's supporters would put up with the way the English game has gone. These changes may have made it the highest-profile league in world football, but it is the fans that have paid most for this rise, both financially and in many other ways. The French would have rioted and burned their stadiums down. German fans would have boycotted matches, but not before unveiling a few pithy banners decrying modern football.

I worry sometimes whether we will always follow this routine. Whether the football is simply a conduit for a social life, for going to the pub. I fear that at some point in the not-too-distant future, we will drift away from going to matches, one by one. As you get older, some of us are becoming less compliant, and more jaded at the hoops we must jump through. I am already hearing murmurings from friends that going to a match is not what it used to be. But I need this routine, and the safety blanket of a routine. I don't like change, in any form.

I wonder how much nostalgia clouds our judgment though. Look, I've already said this, but it feels worth repeating. I fell in love with football in the 1980s, and it was a grim time to be a football fan. If you fall in love with the sport during that decade, then you should be set for life. Tragedy, hooliganism, crumbling grounds, Thatcher's Britain, in which football fans were viewed as scum. ID cards, half-empty grounds, European bans, and more. The Taylor report that resulted from the Hillsborough tragedy was necessary, but then the Premier League happened, money became king, everything became sanitised and that's still better for me than what we had in the 1980s, but it has sucked some of the enjoyment away for many of the old-timers. This is the price of progress though, and things change. We have to change too.

It seems an oxymoron for fans to be falling out of love with the game just as their team is the best they have ever experienced. Some fans are lost in an era of nostalgia, where everything was better in the old days, in their heads. Some are just jaded by life, and for many of us, we're older, wiser, and we have other commitments. Sometimes life takes over. Sometimes, it's feels like a drag.

Can football really be a drag? I see people on Twitter dreaming of their first trip to their team's ground. Fans travel half way across the world for a weekend in Manchester, and their excitement is off the scale. And here's me, forcing myself to the ground sometimes. Thing is, it's not the same for me. I don't know how to work out how many times I have been to a City game, but I will take a rough guess and plump for a round thousand or so. Naturally, entering the Etihad does not have the same allure for me as it may for others. It's part of my weekly routine, like getting on a tram, or ordering a takeaway, though the stakes and potential for joy is higher. And when a run of home games comes in quick succession, which happens more when you start winning most of your games, it can impinge on the rest of your life. By the time you have digested and got over a game, another one is imminent. A hardy few would be happy if the football never stopped, but not me – you can have too much of a good thing. In a way, football is too accessible nowadays. I get to watch every minute of every City match, whether I am in the ground or not. It wasn't always like that. City played fewer games, and I didn't get to see them unless I went to the match. Thus when I did go, it felt more special, as they were less frequent occasions. It's become too easy to go to the match because it's what you do, and you forget the privilege of getting to do so. I think the atmosphere suffers partly for this reason. Is it really a privilege anyway? It's a regular sporting event for which purchasing a ticket is straightforward. Watching this team is a privilege, not the ability to attend matches.

To labour the point about repetition. Imagine going to your first match in five years, and how special that will feel. Approaching the ground. The queue at the turnstiles. The walk through the bustling concourse. Finding your seat, and looking out over the beautifully manicured pitch. Imagine the excitement when the teams come out, and then the match begins. And that first roar from the crowd. A sensory overload.

Now imagine you did that every day of the week, and how quickly that excitement would wane. Soon the queue outside the turnstile is simply an annoyance. The crowded concourse stunts your progress. The view from your seat is nothing special. The game is lacklustre. A period of refereeing incompetence wakes the crowd up for a short while. There's a leak in the roof. You've no chance of getting served at the bar at half-time, unless you're prepared to miss a chunk of the 2nd half. The roads are clogged with traffic afterwards, so you're not getting home anytime soon. The trams are rammed, and irregular. They don't run from the ground anyway, not until next year. It's raining, that drizzle that soaks you through.

Obviously I don't go to a game every day. But the hyperbole I use hopefully gets the message across. I am privileged to see this particular team play football every week. But like most things in life, the experience loses its lustre over time. Use a new oven a thousand times, it will lose its shine.

Nil Points

City's Europa League campaign revolves around Portugal, with City seeing off Porto with ease before going out to Sporting on the away goals rule. I want to feel down, but I feel like an imposter supporting a side in a different European competition to the one they began the season in. I get over this defeat, of sorts, pretty quickly. With a title on the line, I can see the advantages of having all of City's eggs in one basket.

There is plenty of stick thrown City's way online for their European campaign, but with my Premier League title race to worry about, I pay little attention. I'm also fine that rival fans wanted City to fail. That is how it should be. Apparently, according to many commentators down the years, English football fans should support all English sides in European competition, which I readily admit is one of the funniest things I have heard in months. I mean, really?

The problem with some media commentators, is that is clear when you watch or listen to them that they have no idea of what it truly like to be a football fan. A life that does not involve playing the game professionally, or sitting in TV studios, or receiving free tickets to games. A life involving playground taunts, rollercoaster rides, joy and anguish and a life formed in the stands of a football ground with likeminded individuals. So thank you very much for the suggestion, but I will politely decline the opportunity to support all English teams in Europe. And I would hope that non-City fans wish failure on us at every opportunity.

The next day, I start thinking about the nine-year old football stadium I watch my team in. I denigrated the Europa League not because I don't think the competition matters, but because of how City ended up qualifying for it. It just didn't feel right. But when I think about the best atmospheres I have experienced in the short life of this stadium, I realised that they were not necessarily in the biggest competitions. Good atmospheres don't always follow a script, and there is one game that springs to mind. Hamburg at home in the Europa League, a 2-1 win that was not to overturn a 3-1 1st leg deficit, had one of the greatest atmospheres you could hope for, with the tie on a knife edge by the end as City pushed for that extra goal. Hopefully the future will help create many more experiences and new memories are formed in this fairly new location.

The next night, as sleep approaches, out of nowhere comes a vivid football memory. It was 25th May 2005. I was at a friend's house, and she had cooked a selection of tapas, and it was beautiful. I ate until I was almost sick. But that's besides the point. We were gathered for an informal watching of the Champions League final, between Liverpool and AC Milan. As you may know, Liverpool went three goals down in the first half. I found this astonishing, I was mildly amused, but had no strong feelings about Liverpool's woes. Then Liverpool came back with three goals, and I was even more astonished than I was before, but I was not upset. I was enjoying the spectacle of a classic match. Liverpool won on penalties, and perhaps I would rather they had lost, but again, no strong feelings.

If this match played out tomorrow, would I have the same emotions? Nope, I'd be an AC Milan fan for the night. That final was under seven years ago. A lot has changed since then – and it's definitely all the internet's fault.

Go Away

A few days later, after more drinks than I had planned to consume, on an empty stomach, I have the vague memory of a heated debate with my friend Rob about the merits of away goals. Rob is a United supporter so says I am just bitter because City fell foul of the rule. Not true, I have always despised it. It was a rule brought in to make football more entertaining, many decades ago. But does the most popular sport in the world need to be made more entertaining? Did we not all fall in love with the beautiful game because of what it already was? I agree there is a need for some tinkering as times change, and the eradication of the back pass rule was a welcome change, but apart from that, there are no need for much more. And my argument rests on one point above all else - the away goals rule is demonstrably unfair. I am not convinced it has made the sport more entertaining anyway, but if two teams score the same number of goals over two games, why should one team progress, and the other be knocked out? It's rubbish, and I hate it.

I saw an opinion piece writer comment that the joy of the away goals rule is the drama it can present as one goal can mean a team that was losing is now winning. I would use that same situation as absolute proof of its unfairness. One goal should never count for more than one goal. If you are losing a game and score a goal, then the best situation should be that you are now drawing. I cannot see any logic for this not being the case. If we really thought football was not entertaining enough, then we wouldn't be such passionate followers of the sport, and let's just have rubber foam hands for the keepers, moving goals, power plays and random exploding balls. Actually, now I come to think of it, that sounds pretty fun. Away goals can remain in the bin, however.

Doctor Doctor

I am seeing my GP because I have persistent foot pain. Gout say all my friends, though I prefer to suggest plantar fasciitis, an ailment prevalent in athletes. Who am I kidding? The doctor asks me some lifestyle questions, and naturally I lie. It's hard to pin down what I drink, because I am a social imbiber, and it varies wildly according to what I have planned any given week. The more games City play, the more I drink.

Being a match-going football fan is bad for my health. The social life that surrounds it, by which I mean drinking beer, means I am heavier and unhealthier than I would be if I was not a sports fan. I don't drink at home, and I have a more active social life because of the football family I am a part of.

The truth is, the joy of the social life around football for me is more about the "craic" than the units of alcohol consumed. I would happily nurse one pint for three hours if need be, and have done many a time when nursing a hangover or feeling under the weather. The enjoyment of the football match itself is not dependent on being steaming drunk, though on away days home and abroad, it does tend to be part of the deal, and can even make the match an inconvenience.

I go to a lot of comedy and music gigs, and I would hate to be cold sober for any of those events. I think it helps to loosen your inhibitions. But I have been to plenty of football matches with no alcohol in my body and the experience was not wildly different. My enjoyment relies on what happens on the pitch. As I get older, I am beginning to lean more on the company and emotional experience of football, and less on the need to bounce off walls when I eventually depart the pub.

I also despise exercise almost as much as I despise washing pots. I play some squash, wearing a City shirt if they have won the previous weekend, and walk a bit, and that is enough for me. I tried jogging at my sister's suggestion, I really did. I went out early in the morning, because I was so self-conscious. I've seen what some joggers look like, the ones for whom running is not natural. Anyway, I gave it a go, and I lasted three days. Every second was hell. So I guess I have to accept my lot. Football is not going to add years to my life, but the opposite.

Or will it? Being surrounded by friends on a regular basis cannot be a bad thing, whatever the location. Mental health is as important as physical health, and my matchday routine, and much of what surrounds it (arguing online apart) is good for me, good for all of us. You can see its benefit when you're sat there, round a table, different conversations dancing in the air. Shuttling off to the bar, spending a penny, a quick smoke for some. Picking up where we left off. Dividing us into our separate taxis to the ground. And then we will do the same thing next week. Creatures of habit.

Happy Birthday

It's dad's birthday, and I don't know what to get him. I like giving presents, apart from the financial strain it places on me, but on this occasion, I wonder what I could possibly get him that he could appreciate. He was always a man without any hobbies, only now he is a man without much of a memory or concentration span too.

All I can think is that it would be nice to get something for his room, so for the first time in my life I buy some flowers for a man, and a small painting to hang up. It's by a local artist, and portrays a snowy scene in a street of terraced houses. The kids play, the mums look on. There is a pub on a corner, emitting a golden glow from within, and I can almost taste its atmosphere.

A nurse helps me hang up the painting when my dad is in the toilet. When he eventually returns, I show him the painting. He expresses genuine joy when he sees it, and says it reminds him of a street near where he grew up in north Manchester. We stand there for a while, talking about the painting and him growing up.

My sister has bought him a subscription to a motoring magazine, and a big box of chocolates. There are plenty of cards stood up on the windowsill, far more than I get nowadays. That's fine, there's not a single person in the pub on a matchday that has ever sent a card to anyone else.

We have a piece of birthday cake, and then dad gets sleepy. I say my goodbyes, and sit in the car, engine off, for a fair amount of time. I should cherish these moments, but they only serve to make me sad. On this special day, I am feeling grief for someone who is still alive.

Life Art

My foot is still giving me bother. My GP didn't seem to know what it is, so suggests rest. There's no time to. I limp to the next game, and as the final whistle goes, I try to avoid the crowds and let my row empty out before joining the throngs streaming out of the stadium. I am going to get a taxi into town and meet friends in the pub. The situation reminds me of a strange ambition I have. One day, I would love to stay in my seat until everyone else has left.

In theory I have already had this experience. I have been in a corporate box twice, and they are a great experience once every blue moon, though inappropriate personally for an important match. There would be a conflict in doing so, between the stress of a big match, and the relaxation and decadence that is a natural part of the corporate experience. The first time I was invited to a corporate box, I had no idea what the experience entailed, and not did the person who invited me, himself a guest on behalf of a betting company. We both agreed that it was unlikely free food would be part of the deal, so we ate before arriving, at which point we discovered that the evening included a four-course meal. I'm ashamed to admit I ate every morsel. The baffling thing was, I woke up the next morning really, really hungry. The night took me back to childhood, when McDonalds ran a Trivial Pursuit scratch card competition, the prizes mostly being free food. Every night I used to stock up on chips and cheeseburgers on my way home, at which point I would then have my normal evening meal.

Being in a box means remaining behind after the match, as the food and refreshments continues to flow, so you get the partial experience of seeing the ground empty, but usually whilst distracted by other goings on. What I will do instead one day is sit in my seat and watch everyone go by. Listen as the noise dissipates. And when ready, make a leisurely exit from the ground. As the vendors pack up and the final stragglers make their way from the ground.

It's a rather bizarre thing to have on your bucket list. Partly because I doubt anyone else in the planet counts it as a life ambition, and partly because it's so easily attainable. I'm usually with someone at a match though, so the obligation to leave when the match ends (or before) is too great.

Lives Collide

While I may miss the occasional game due to a prior engagement, my family know that no social arrangements can be made without consulting the fixture list. Quite simply, if City are playing on any given day, I am not available. They know that my commitment to my team extends beyond 90 minutes. It is the pub, the travel, the debate, and more. A game takes up my day. What's more, a busy day may mean the following morning is out of bounds too.

What are you prepared to miss in order to watch your team play? A gig, a wedding, or more? The importance of the game matters, but for a select few, a game cannot be missed. For the very select few, every game must be attended, not just watched. I can never reach those levels of fandom, and am happy not to. Whilst football does control much of my life, I'd miss out on too much of the other stuff that life has to offer if I ramped up that control any further.

"I've looked at the dates, and the weekend of the 19th seems the best time to go and visit Mark and Sam."
"The 19th?"
"Yes. I checked the fixture list, and you're not playing that weekend."
"Ah."
"What?! You're clearly not playing."
"Well, not at the moment, no."
"What's that supposed to mean?"
"It's a blank weekend, set aside for FA Cup 4th round fixtures."
"Are City in that?"
"They're in the 3rd round. If they win, then they will have a game that weekend."
"Who have they got?"

"Mansfield at home."

"I don't know where Mansfield is, so I have a feeling they're not very good."

"You'd be right with that assessment."

"Oh for fuck's sake. I give up. Which day would they be playing on?"

"Could be the Saturday. Or the Sunday. Or the Friday, or the Monday."

"Well, when will you know?"

"After the 3rd round, then the 4th round draw, then when the TV companies announce the live games."

"When will that be?"

"In about a month?"

"I can't wait that long. I need to book train tickets."

"Well, that's just how it is. I can't speed it up."

"And the game is more important than seeing friends for the first time in nine months?"

"I'm not saying that. I mean I don't know who we're playing yet."

"You know what, forget it. I'll go by myself. Enjoy your sodding football match. "

Happiness Happening

Claire used to pick me up on this quite a lot.

"You don't seem very happy being a football fan?"

And she was right, though perhaps she missed my happy moments, and instead caught me at my worst, getting worked up at something I considered unfair on the internet. Or sulking for 24 hours after a bad result. The moments of pure joy were mostly experienced away from her presence.

My team have risen to the level where they are competing for a Premier League title. Not just competing, they're top of the table right not. Any outsider would logically assume I would be happy about this. And yet I am not. I am fidgety, nervous, on edge. Anxious, worried. I can keep perusing the Thesaurus for more descriptions if necessary, but you get the idea.

Is football too competitive? Has all the money meant there is too much at stake, including for fans? Yes I am nervous by nature, and a natural worrier. Even so, I should be able to extract some joy from a title race. This team is amazing, the best I have ever watched. Ultimately, the joy comes at full time, after a good result. Then it's back to the grind, studying the league table and analysing fixture lists. After that whistle, after a good result – there can be no drug on earth that replicates the feeling. It sustains you as a fan.

Claire took no interest in football. In fact, she hated it. I took her to one game, that predictably ended 0-0, and accepted that I would never change her mind. I had no particular desire to, as I had no need for her to be involved in my main passion in life. But I at least hoped that by softening her attitude, it could help our relationship, and help her understand why I do what I do, and why I feel what I feel. I failed, and that barrier remained.

In Fever Pitch, at one point Nick Hornby shouts "you don't understand!" to his girlfriend about his passion for football and the inevitable moods that accompanied it. I once shouted the same at Claire, but the truth is, I didn't understand either. To this day, I still don't. I can't put it into words with any clarity why it all matters so much. Football has never been logical, and I should stop trying to figure it all out.

I've taken five people to a game in order to show to them what football is about. City didn't win any of the games. It is time to accept that I am not a football missionary, and don't need to be. I once took a United-supporting friend to watch City play Blackpool at Bloomfield Road. An abysmal match was not helped by the bright winter sun that blinded us throughout, and at half-time there was a lottery draw, for which the 3rd place prize was an egg and cress sandwich. My friend said little after the match. He could have really rubbed in what he had witnessed. His team was wining league titles and challenging for European trophies. My team was lumping the ball up field in the 3rd tier of English football, stumbling from one disaster to another. I think he stayed quiet because he pitied me, because it felt like this was how it was always going to be. There wasn't even a rivalry anymore. As I wasted money on a fruit machine in a grotty pub on the sea front, I remember him saying that he hoped that City returned to the Premier League one day, as it was not the same without having that rivalry. It felt patronising, but he was being sincere. Careful what you wish for I replied, and we both laughed, knowing City would probably never be the best team in Manchester. I made him a promise that day. If City ever win the First Division, I'd get a tattoo of United's club crest on my backside, and raise some money for the Christie Hospital. I wonder if he remembers me saying that?

It was January 1999. It's been a long journey. But there's now a chance. I wonder if my friend is glad of the rivalry. I guess that's a question to be answered at the end of the season.

A Life Without Sport

Claire had little interest in any sport, and I wonder what that is like. I cannot imagine such a life. Sport thrills me, in almost all its forms. I can pass a weekend watching sport. I can flick instantly from the drama of a football match to the tension at the end of a cricket one-day international. Consume myself in weeks of Olympic action. Stay up late into the night to watch action from the other side of the world. If it doesn't involve dancing horses, I'm all in.

Without sport, I'd need something to else to give me that buzz, and to take up much of my spare time. And there's nothing else that would come close. I consume TV, books and films, and all three have made me cry, laugh, and brought me joy and anger, but it's a different feeling compared to what your team makes you feel. Not necessarily better or worse, just different. Never as intense. Nothing can stir your emotions like your favourite sports team.

The number of mornings I have woken up and wished I was one of those people that was not ruled by sport. A day watching boxsets without a knot in your stomach. I just don't need the stress, I never do. Take the easy way out, that has always been my way. A cancelled game brings me relief rather than annoyance. Sometimes you may wonder whether I even like the sport I profess to hold an obsession for, as Claire often asked.

The match itself is not always that bad. It is the build-up, the long day, the agonising wait, the tense moment when the team sheet is announced, the concern over whether it is the right team, because naturally you know better than the manager. And then that hour that remains until kick off. Torture for the big games.

Once the game begins, the stress does not disappear, but at least now you will know one way or another within a couple of hours whether this has been a great or terrible day. At least now you are occupied with the match, rather than pacing around your house getting little if any work done. The not knowing is as bad as the knowing, even if the knowing brings bad news.

Being a sports fan doesn't suit cautious people. You can control other aspects of your life. Don't take the risk of trying for a promotion, risking a new challenge, no asking out the woman you think about every day. Nope, avoid that, and settle for a life of safety and anonymity. You sign up for sport, you have lost that control. Fortunes are now in the hands of others. Or feet, to be precise.

Celebration Police

The celebration police are out on Twitter. They always are, to be fair. No cuts to their budget, they patrol the football grounds of England, and its video content, 24/7. There is this section of football fans that like to portray themselves as true supporters despite the evidence to the contrary, that love to decide how fans should celebrate goals and results. It's part of the football sub-genre where everything is a competition, not just the football itself. Everything must be rated, essentially so that some things can be derided. Across message boards and social media, they use these celebrations, or lack of, as a mechanism to increase divides across fan bases. And as social media becomes more and more a part of many of our lives, then tribalism will grow with it, and this situation will only become worse. It is just one of the unsavoury aspects of fandom that only exist in modern times. I'll try not to sink into pointless nostalgia, but occasionally I pine for the days when the Football Pink was the sole arbiter of how a team had played that day. Having said that, as the internet grew and I got to see every kick of every ball made by my football team, I soon realised how inaccurate the match reports in the national newspapers could be, and how they may have warped the perception of the competence of my team. Nostalgia is overrated anyway.

Family Time

I go and see dad, and take some Thornton chocolates. He really likes chocolates. He is not in his bedroom, which I am always glad to discover. I hate the thought of him being imprisoned in there, but the staff here are wonderful, and do what they can to help him experience a basic level of normality. He is sat in a deep chair, looking out over the grounds. There are sycamore and oak trees, and a squirrel bounds across the lawn. The sun is breaking through the clouds. It's a typical day of UK weather, when there is no real weather to speak of. The TV is on and other residents watch Escape To The Country.

Dad is distant today, so I sit there and little is said. These are the times that I get my guilty thoughts. Thoughts about me not needing to be here, and that I could be doing something else instead. That if he does not understand what is going on, then what is the point? And I know this is wrong, but I cannot stop these fleeting thoughts. At least they are fleeting. It's not as if I have anything else of importance to attend to. And the nurse has assured me that my dad knows I am there, and that it helps. I guess that away from my own selfishness, I just feel helpless about it all. Watching someone fade away before your eyes makes me not only feel sorrow for my dad, but for myself at having to endure this. I'm being selfish again.

The nurse's name is Joy, and she is a hero to me, for what she does for my dad. She can read me like a book too.

"If you want to go, don't feel guilty. Your dad will be glad you were here, however long."

I always bring dad a magazine, for what it is worth. He was – is – fascinated by military history, so I have left him something about the First World War, and how it started. It is unlikely he will ever read a single word.

Seeing my dad forces me to confront my mortality. With my mum bravely battling cancer for so many years, I wonder about the balance of wanting to live and quality of life. But then as a family we are all petrified of death, as our lack of religious convictions ensures we do not see anything beyond it, so it is tradition to try and hang on for as long as is possible.

There's something else bothering me though. My dad's life is fading, it shows on every part of his face, but there's still a twinkle in his eye when we talk about City, when he is capable of doing so. He knows City are in a title race. That should make me happy, if I didn't I feel like my dad is hanging on, to see if City can win the league. That once they have, he has lived his life, and there is nothing left to give. If they do win the title, would I even be brave enough to tell him?

I take my dad out and about sometimes too. Not too often, as he can get very unsettled with new situations. I take him to Morecambe but it rains and we sit in the car eating sandwiches, looking out to sea. We have always been drawn to the coast. My mum insisted that the sea air was good for our skin.

The Tide Turns

It feels like City are relentless in the league, but so are the team across town, and it only takes one match for the tide to turn and the wheels to fall off. City lose 1-0 at Swansea City, not a game I had bookmarked as a banana skin. For the first time in five months, City are not top of the league. Will they be top again?

The Swansea defeat predictability hits me hard. Sleep is fitful, at best. I do not help my wellbeing by repeatedly dipping into social media to remind myself how badly every other City fan seems to be taking the result. There is no credible reason for me doing this, the online equivalent of rubbernecking at an accident. I know what happened, I know what went wrong, who played badly, and the challenges that lie ahead. Reading other fans bemoaning everything that went wrong serves no purpose. And yet I keep going back, as if embracing masochism. I want to hurt more. It is certainly not proving cathartic, and it makes my mind race further, delaying sleep until late into the night. The next day is close to a write-off. I shout out a lot of stupid stuff, impulsively, at matches, we all do, but Twitter seems to be the online equivalent, where instead of words being lost in the breeze, they are recorded for all to see, in perpetuity. Some of the comments would have you think City had been relegated, and I fall into a brief period of despondency. Unhealthy food is my refuge, not for the first time.

I'm down on my team, but this is nothing compared to what used to happen. For a couple of years in my 20s, when temping at an accountant firm and taking any other work that kept my head above water, I lived on the next street to Maine Road. At my house warming party, a couple of United-supporting friends thought it funny to go and urinate on the side of the stadium. Because I was steaming drunk, and City were a poor side at the time, I joined them. It was my crude way of sticking two fingers up at the team that was causing me so much pain, though naturally I regretted my actions the following morning.

If on the off chance you're reading this and not a big football fan, we're not all like this. A friend of a friend was in the pub to watch the defeat, and I was struck by how soon after full time he had forgotten the match had even happened. He is a City fan, always has been, goes to a few games, but not every week. Bottom line is, football does not rule his life. Those with a casual interest in the sport are looked down upon by many die-hard fans. Many passionate fans think that an interest in football must be all or nothing. Either throw your life and emotions into your football team, or try another sport. Spend half your earnings on following your football club, have your club crest tattooed on your shin and never miss a match or else don't bother. Having said all that, there are plenty of home and away attendees that can also swat away the misery of a bad result in no time. They sit in a pub after a match and chastise me for having a face "like a slapped arse".

Grading levels of football support is not fair, is it? There's no rule book on how to follow a football club. No obligation on how serious to take it all. I almost envy casual fans. They can walk away when things aren't great and get on with their lives, but still experience the glory of success. But is their rollercoaster ride each season a gentler affair? Would a league title or FA Cup triumph resonate as much with them? Only they can answer that.

Personally, I find it easier to deal with a season that never really takes off compared to a season that promises plenty before tailing off, even if the end result is identical. False hope can be damaging, but with the former, you find peace quickly once you realise it is not to be. Knowing early doors that the season is going to disappoint at least allows you to adapt, and get on with your life, without being strung along.

Twitterati

Another day spending too long on Twitter. Hate it, will never leave it.

Today's Twitter thought: I'm not sure the angst over failure used to be this severe. Social media is clearly playing a huge part. Everything is magnified and exacerbated. Everyone fuels everyone else, like a perpetual motion machine. There's no stopping it now, an immovable force.

Football fans love to take credit for their own team's success, as they see the team as an extension of themselves. Another by-product of this is the need to over-defend their club, hold blinkered viewpoints and struggle with any perceived failure. And I have noticed a new trend, which is weird as City have lost so few games this season. The trend is to rewrite history after a bad result. Everyone was on top of the world just a couple of weeks ago, as City challenged for their first ever league title, a challenge not everyone predicted. A bad result is all it takes to re-evaluate the squad and question the recruitment policy over the past few years. Win next week, and everything is fine again. Everything in football is so binary on there. Success or failure, with nothing in between. I've seen a club crucified for finishing 2nd in a 20-team league. Where is the nuance?

My time online has made me notice the rise of fan media, that is surely only going to grow and grow in the coming years. How it will develop, and what paths it will take, I do not know. I contribute occasionally to a podcast, which I do partly as therapy. A way to come out of my shell and not hide behind a screen all my life. With our short attention spans and the unstoppable spread of online content over print content, expect short-form output to become king. It's nice to hear thoughts from supporters of your own club, the ones that know best what is right and what is wrong, but already I can see that not everyone is happy at such a shift in what is being put out there. That's because such fans dare have differing opinions to them, and it's hard for many to accept.

I can't sit on my high horse here, as I am no better. Spending time online has seen me develop a second personality, and not a nice one. I am a different person, as are many people, as the form of communication is different. We are more aggressive, ruder, and more tribal when we communicate remotely. And I have found myself getting upset at fellow fans for being critical of City players, or any aspect of the club because I simply don't agree. As if everyone must happy-clap and see the positive and my club must be protected at all times. It is ridiculous, and it is not healthy.

Differing opinions are fine, as is constructive criticism. Some fans seem to think that the actions of other fans who support the same club bring shame on them, and whilst I can see why they would think that, as a fanbase is in some way a family, I do not really agree. We are all responsible for our own actions, and them alone. If my uncle went on a killing spree, there is no reason why that should paint me in a bad light. And if your club is being criticised, that does not reflect badly on you. You did not do anything wrong.

Best Team In The Land?

City may have hit a rocky patch, but this is still the best team I have had the privilege to watch. Critics may argue the competition has not always been particularly stiff. City have had many, many average players during my lifetime. And yet I sit here, typing away, unwilling to slag them off, or call them rubbish. Many fellow blues will say that is precisely what they were, but I cannot do it. They may well have not been good enough even for an underachieving Manchester City side, but they must have been pretty good at football to get that far in their careers, even if my eyes suggested otherwise. If they tried their best, and you can't ask for more than that, then I don't feel the need long after they have departed to lay into them. I'm sure my opinions were rather different at the time though, as Lee Bradbury scored his 3rd goal of the season in March. The only exception to this rule of not slagging off ex-players is if they did not try, were lazy, and/or their attitude stunk. A fanbase pinned their hopes on these players year after year, and to not put in 100% at least most of the time is inexcusable.

Every football fan, at whatever level their team operates at, has watched a player and wondered how on earth they made it as a professional. Deep down, you know they can't be as bad as what the evidence suggests. Sometimes, it just doesn't work out, and a player stripped of confidence is little better than you and I. Well, perhaps a tad fitter, though during City's nadir I watched the odd City player I was convinced was in worse physical condition than me.

City's old scouting method was rather flawed, as it appeared to be based on signing players who had a good game against us. Jon Macken scored from near the half-way line against City on a wet and windy day at Deepdale, a game Preston North End won 2-1, so City soon signed him, paying ten times his value. Robert "Bob" Taylor was another, a player who, along with myself, required lifestyle tips.

Perspective Returns

With City out of all cup competitions, I have time to lick my wounds before the next match. On 17th March, there's some FA Cup action, but I am more interested in a comedy gig in Manchester. As I catch a pre-gig pint, I pop online with my new phone as I await the arrival of a friend, and my stomach churns at what I read. At White Hart Lane, Bolton Wanderers player Fabrice Muamba has collapsed on the pitch, and it seems he has suffered a cardiac arrest.

I have been at a match and witnessed a player swallow their tongue during a match, and it was naturally a horrible experience. It plays on my mind the crowd having to go through that, though that pales into insignificance compared to what Muamba himself endured.

I go off to the gig, not sure if a Premier League footballer is going to survive the night. I feel nauseous. As it turns out, Muamba's heart stopped for 78 minutes. But miraculously, he survives.

Fabrice Muamba will surely never play professional football again. But on a sad night, what is most important is that he is here to tell the tale. He gets to live his life, and see his wife and children every day. And they get to live their life with a father and husband as part of that. So despite everything, I go to bed thankful.

Thankfully the match itself was abandoned by referee Howard Webb, as was Bolton's next match three days later against Aston Villa. It is welcoming to see that we appear to have moved on and realised protecting the "product" is not the primary concern in situations like this. After the Heysel tragedy, and I mean immediately after 39 people were crushed to death, the match went ahead. It is staggering to consider this fact in 2012. They still played the game. I would like to think that this could never happen in the modern world. It hasn't always been this way. The show must go on, however much suffering surrounds the sport. I'm not sure anything short of a nuclear war or worldwide pandemic could halt a football schedule for more than a day or so though.

Pub Talk

"Right. I have almost certainly forgotten somewhere, but I think I've been to 47 grounds. That's pretty poor."

"It is what it is, not a competition. I think I have done 110 or so. I spent my 20s, going home and away, racked up a lot in that time."

"Here's a follow-up question. How many no longer exist?"

"Jeez, quite a few. Burnden Park, Maine Road obviously, The Dell, Highbury, Goldstone Ground, Saltergate..."

"Oh yeah, forgot that one. Probably because I've seen City draw and lose there.."

"You doused your chips in salt when the lid fell off. Highlight of the night. Ninian Park, Vetch Field, the old Wembley, Filbert Street, Baseball Ground, I could go on for a bit longer I reckon."

"What about abroad? Six for me. Driven past another 50 or so though."

"I will guess at about 15. Two in Germany, Spain, Denmark, got to factor in a couple of England games and pre-season tours."

"Ok then, best away?"

"Got to be Aalborg, Denmark. Crazy two days, what I remember of it. You?"

"Not been to many, so not much to compare. But watching football in Germany is always the best. So Schalke trip I guess."

"Good trip, except for David missing the flight home."

"He probably shouldn't have spent the night in a Cologne brothel then..."

"Allegedly."

"Yeah, maybe his phone made its own way there."

"These new smartphones can do anything nowadays."

Life Fails To Imitate Art

I spend a lazy Sunday barely moving, as marathon runners pass my window, adding to my guilt. I lie on the couch watching sport for so long that my TV goes into rest mode three times. Flicking through the channels, I notice Escape To Victory, and that's another 90 minutes taken care of.

Have you ever seen a football match perfectly replicated on the big screen? It can be painful to watch football in a TV drama or film. In some ways it's an impossible task, because how do you transport viewers to the moments we as fans have all felt? How can a viewer possibly feel the same way from something that is not real, and not live? They can't, not that Escape To Victory is really the best example to use.

In an era when United swept up trophies whilst their neighbours stumbled from one mishap to another, seeing United humbled, mocked and experience any form of ignominy on screen was often as good as it got. Tiny victories. I dream, optimistically of the roles being reversed one day. Picking on City's flaws off the pitch because there's little to criticise on it.

A film that encapsulated this better than any was the 2000 release of "There's Only One Jimmy Grimble". At this time, City were an upward curve, but it was a curve that began from a very low base, at the same time Manchester United were winning a treble. If you are not aware of this modern masterpiece, it is about a City-supporting schoolkid, who is bullied, and your typical movie underdog. The school bully is in the school's football team, holding back Jimmy's own progress, despite his clear talent. Needless to say it all turns out OK, and Jimmy's footballing prowess attracts the attention of professional scouts, culminating in this famous dialogue:

Manchester United scout: "How would you like to join us at Man United?"

Jimmy: "Very nice of you, but I've got a better offer."
Manchester United scout: "What could be better than Man United, son?"
Jimmy: "Man City!"

Hardly the greatest burn in movie history, but when you're feeding on scraps, you take it. Still, it pales into insignificance compared to the tirade that Jim Broadbent lets forth in an episode of the drama series The Street, directed at a table of United fans in a pub. A series penned by Jimmy McGovern, who just happens to be from Liverpool. Despite my obvious desire, fuelled by tribalism, to watch the scene with a grin on my face, Broadbent's (McGovern's) comments that the Munich Air Disaster was the best thing that ever happened to United as no one gave a damn about them before then, does not sit comfortably with me. There may be some truth in a tragedy having such consequences for a football team, but it is not a discussion I ever feel the need to take part in. Jimmy McGovern clearly disagrees.

Happy Birthday To Me

Birthdays don't matter to me anymore. But it's mine, so I have to go through the routine. Saying thanks on Facebook, and trying not to think about my own mortality. All these memories will not exist one day, they go with me. Happy birthday!

As a child, it was a very different situation, and you approached the big day with anticipation, with enough hints offered in previous weeks about what you wanted. For a football-obsessed child, there were two obvious items that I cherished above all else. An actual football, which should need no explanation. I mean, just holding one, even now, feels wonderful. Truth be told, I can say that about a lot of sporting equipment. Holding a squash racquet and swooshing it through the air gives me great satisfaction. A snooker cue is a thing of beauty. Prodding a cricket bat into the ground, the smack of leather on willow, that most exquisite of sounds. A ten-pin bowling ball, if I can find one that accommodates my fat fingers. All these things and more thrill me.

My second prized possession, just below my mountain bike, was Subbuteo. There was a Games Workshop store in the centre of Manchester that I would visit with glee, when I had collected enough pocket money. There was one corner set aside for Subbuteo, and it was a way to discover about football not just in England, or the UK, but the whole world. I didn't want another City team, I wanted Slavia Prague in their away kit. I wanted exotic kits with sashes. I wanted the scoreboard, stands around the pitch and spectators too. I wanted to create my own world, and let my imagination run wild. I wanted to be transported around the globe from my own bedroom. I'm not sure I even enjoyed the game itself that much, but more everything that came with it. I've always been a dreamer, and this was a great way to facilitate that.

There was plenty more football memorabilia as I grew up. The Panini sticker albums, the thrill of a new packet, soon dashed by getting Peter Beardsley for the 12th time. I had a board game called Wembley, based on the 1981 FA Cup campaign, which as a City fan was unfortunate as it ended in such heartache. Then there were my tournament wallcharts, early computer games and I even had a watch in my teens that had a football game on it. It took me 3 hours to master it, but I played it for a year.

No more. I watch football, I write about it, I talk about it, and that is it. I don't play football games on my Playstation or PC, not since the heady days of Championship Manager 92 and International Superstar Soccer on my Nintendo 64. I tried playing a game online once, and was thrashed 6-0 by a 12-year-old. Never again.

There is no card from Claire, and I don't know how this makes me feel. Sad, I guess, though I should not have expected one. Our lives are separate now, and always will be.

To Absent Friends

I am not good with names. This can be problematic. I recall my friend telling me that Paul had died from a heart attack. Who is Paul, I asked, before being informed it was the bloke who had sat behind me at the ground for much of the past three years. We'd talked a lot, but never introduced ourselves to each other, that I can remember. I never saw him outside the ground, and sadly now I never will.

Paul was a Jekyll and Hyde character at matches. When things were going badly, he was unbearable at times, a tirade of abuse and moaning. One bad half and the entire team needed to be shipped out, the manager sacked, the board gone. Our recruitment was pathetic, and serious questions needed to be asked. When things were going well, he was a different person. Believed that City were going to rule the world, and there was no stopping them. There was no nuance with Paul. And he may have annoyed me at times, to the point that I once walked around the concourse for 10 minutes to escape him, but he was part of the football family, he was part of the matchday experience. There will be a hole where his seat is. But someone else will come along and fill that hole, and the cycle continues. One day, someone will sit in my seat for the first time, and begin a new journey.

Changing Times

Throughout the book I have written about men. That's what our group has traditionally been. A group of very non-diverse men. Perhaps such a group does not feel welcoming or appealing to a woman. Perhaps even threatening? We are the least threatening group around, but I understand why others may not see that. Maybe we're just boring. I've never given it much thought until I started writing this book, because everyone has always been welcome, and this is how the cards fell.

It's still a sport attended by mostly males. Even fans as a collective are referred to as male – we are the Twelfth Man, after all. What did I say at the beginning about supporting the same team as your dad, and his dad? No one ever says mother. In times of old, crowds had a similar make up. Thankfully times are changing. On a match day, women, men, children come and go at whichever pub we set up camp at. And the ground is awash with every variety of human, as it should be.

Bizarrely, you can see the angst that progress creates with some old-timers. They're almost threatened by change. Threatened by anyone who isn't a near-clone of themselves.

Through The Ages

Stuart is in a foul mood for some reason, and no one is keen to ask him why. He is musing over whether this is our life now, sitting in pubs and going to the match until we die. If so, I reply, what is wrong with that? But then I add that we are not in our final lap as a football fan, hopefully, as long as we lay off those pork scratchings and go for a walk occasionally. No, there is one more lap after this one for us. You see, the four of us currently in the pub on this sunny Manchester day are in our 4th age as a football fan, and I explain to the other three how you can split all fans up this way, not that they asked me to.

My first age as a fan would have been a young child, the period when I feel in love with football, and experienced it all with wide-eyed wonder. By the end of this first age, I would have been old enough to understand what was going on with my club properly, and as a sensitive child (and adult), this would probably have involved quite a lot of crying. If this had been in the age of Sky Sports, I'm likely to have been the kid the cameras would pan in on after a painful and damaging defeat, using my scarf as a tissue. I don't have a detailed memory of childhood, apart from it being comfortable and fun, but I have a vague memory of the tears flowing after England's defeat in Italia 90. I recall me in full England kit, walking up to my room after the agony of penalties, and blubbing for a good while. Perhaps this was the first time that I lost the innocence of youth. When you're a child, football is fun and sparkly and loud and exciting. Then you reach an age when it dawns on you for the first time. Football is indeed amazing, it is everything, but it can break your heart like your first proper girlfriend. It can build up your hopes and smash them to pieces in an instant. If you support certain clubs, it seems almost inevitable. If you support England, definitely so.

And the first age of my journey would have provided ample opportunity for tears. City were a side who struggled to reach any peaks after their relegation in 1983, when a late Raddy Antic goal consigned City to the 2nd tier of English football. City would come back up, but then in 1987 go back down again, before another promotion saw a limited period of stability in the top division under Peter Reid, as the Premier League era dawned in 1992.

My second age as a football fan was the teenage years. In many ways, this is the most exciting time to be a supporter. A coming of age, the true excitement of standing on a terrace, the introduction of alcohol, and your first away day, at least as an adult, and perhaps without family but with friends instead. True adventures, a true belonging.

Sadly, this period coincided with my football team being truly shit. City fans had got rid of Peter Swales, as they wrongly believed that Francis Lee would bring the good times back to Maine Road. We were wrong, as was Lee's belief that his friend Alan Ball would make a good manager. City were relegated in 1996, in true City style. Holding the ball in the corner when drawing with Liverpool, on the false understanding that they only needed a point to stay up. Out of the dressing room ran a partially-dressed Niall Quinn, who had earlier been substituted, to tell the City players they needed to win, but by then it was too late. Within a couple of years, City were playing in the third tier of English football for the first time in their history.

The third age of my football fandom was thankfully a brighter affair. This age is about young adulthood, primarily being a supporter in your 20s. You still have your youth, but you feel wiser too, and invincible. Only when a friend died in his mid-30s a decade or so later would I lose that feeling.

City won the 1999 play-off final against Gillingham, after Paul Dickov's last-gasp equaliser. Another promotion followed, a relegation, and then a promotion. City would slowly become an established Premier League side, as Kevin Keegan brought flair and excitement back to the club, after Joe Royle had steadied the ship. And in 2003, the move from Maine Road, a sad day, but the price of progress. Who knows how different City's history may have been in they had remained at their old ground.

And so to the present day. I am now in my fourth age of being a football fan. I categorise this age as being in my 30s and 40s. The mid-life. My body has started aching for no reason, and the hair is greying. Vision is not the best, and I've long retired from the five-a-side circuit as I get too frustrated at my body's limitations. There are 70-year-olds still playing, but then they are fitter than me. I'm at that age now where I walk into a room and have no idea why I did it, until I leave the room, when I immediately remember. But I am truly wise now, a City elder, of sorts. That's how we see ourselves anyway, all of us. I have been there and done it, I have paid my dues and have earned any success that may come my team's way now, unlike the young whipper-snappers who have only known relatively good times, and are likely to have a much smoother ride ahead of them compared to my first three ages.

And for the fourth age, it's been some ride. A new stadium, and then the lull before the storm. Kevin Keegan imploded because it's what he does, though to be fair he was not backed with signings, probably because the pot was once more empty. The lull was the Stuart Pearce years, when you could go months without seeing a goal. Then a corrupt Thai ex-Prime Minister took over, we soon understood the smoke and mirrors that defined his year in charge, and suddenly, without warning, we were the richest club in the world. Now we have won something, and the future is bright. It's been emotional.

Hopefully, the fifth age is the longest. I'm hoping to reach national life expectancy averages. I guess this is the age my dad is at, though neither of us pictured it ending this way. But the fifth age is old age, however you wish to define that. The grumpiness that has crept into me, about life in general and not just football, may intensify in my final age, or hopefully ebb away as I come to accept my own mortality, and try to make the most of what is left. And with old age, I would hope I am no longer the sort of person who sits on social media arguing about what defines a big club. Perhaps instead I will be in the garden, with a nice cup of tea, wondering if we ever got the most out of Samir Nasri. Sat in a home, reminiscing about the class of 2012.

I wonder what football I will witness? Money rules in football, and my club has loads of it, so perhaps a golden age lies ahead. Football is also cyclical however, so there must be lean times. I hope I am philosophical by this point, as any period of competing at the top would provide more silverware than many football fans get to see in a lifetime.

All I will say is that if you live your second age during a period when your team is successful, never take it for granted. Always be thankful, because you are living the dream. I do not know what the future holds, but the takeover of my club in 2008 clearly indicates that some success is almost inevitable, the opposite of what I grew up expecting. I hoped for some success, but not for one moment did I expect it. Any success will be enjoyed whatever our respective ages. But I think as a youngster, there are extra opportunities.

It's What We Do

I wonder if Stuart is losing his enthusiasm for football. Every week, how many fans are going to matches purely out of an obligation to do so, because it's what they have always done? For fans of teams who are not playing well, the match-going routine is a struggle. Many of us with season tickets will have sat at a match, wondering if maybe this was the last time we will make that commitment, as the experience is not what it was. I mean, if the team can't be bothered, why should I?

And then we renew our season ticket again.

Or most of us do. As City have risen, some fans have still fallen. A team's success does not demand attendance. People have other things going on in their lives, and going to a football match every week is not always on the list of priorities. One friend is struggling with his health, and finds the match-day experience too difficult, too exhausting. Another friend picks and chooses matches because he has young twins to occupy his time. Another simply misses the old days. Standing, a tension outside the ground, the ramshackle nature of it all, not being viewed as a consumer. Eventually we will all go to a match for the final time, for different reasons.

Making A Difference

I've got a new superstition now, and as always I have no idea why. At home I have a number of half-used aftershaves that take up an entire shelf in my bedroom. I can only assume that after a good result earlier in the season, I remembered the aftershave I put on earlier that day, and I will take an educated guess that it was an aftershave I was wearing for the first time. Thus, it was obviously the aftershave that won City the game, and I now must wear it on every matchday. And the stupid thing is, inevitably City will lose a game when I am wearing that aftershave, but the superstition will continue.

Soon, I am developing the superstition according to game type. I decide, after City lose away, that I need two separate aftershaves, one for home games, one for away games. I am yet to decide on the best course of action for games played at a neutral venue - we'll cross that bridge when we get to it. So I am now on two different aftershaves, and all the others for non-matchdays. When they run out, I will have to decide whether buying a replacement aftershave when I have 17 other ones to use is really a sensible idea, but if it helps City win multiple trophies, then I really have little choice.

I choose my aftershave for away games. The following week, City win.

Phew. The title race remains alive. You're welcome.

Elsewhere, the same superstitions remain, as they are clearly having an effect. I do not believe in a god, I follow science, and what I perceive to be logic and reasoning, and yet here I am going through this preposterous routine every single match. Another source of conflict with Claire was her quasi-religious belief in horoscopes, astrology, mediums and the like. I shouldn't have cared, as she is free to believe in what she wants. However, when she once commented that perhaps part of our problem was that two Aires don't go well together in a relationship, I had to bite my lip so forcibly that blood was drawn.

My superstitions were always her go-to argument, and I had no come-back, however bogus astrology clearly is. I have to keep wearing my Adidas Spezials. sky blue, white stripes. They're not comfy, and I've lost my love for the brand, but needs must. I must cross the road I live on at the top, by the lights. The earlier I cross the road, the worse City play. Left turnstile at the ground, up the steps two at a time. Left urinal if possible in the ground, though if I go at half-time, I don't get to choose. I would get some strange looks and perhaps some choice words too if I stood in front of an empty urinal but remained in line as I considered it cursed.

Left sock on first, same jacket now for the rest of the season, irrespective of weather conditions. Left seat by window in pre-match pub, always contribute £2 towards the taxi fare.

Football As A Neutral

There are some fans, that go home and away, that have an obsession of sorts about visiting all 92 grounds in the football league. For many, this can only be achieved by their own team playing at all these grounds, an almost impossible prospect, so it's just a case of ticking off as many as possible. For others, they will attend random matches to complete the task, perhaps as part of their love of football in general, or just to say they've been there. It's an achievement that has become harder to clarify in recent times due to the many teams that have moved into new stadiums. The waters have been muddied, and the 92 teams in the league changes, naturally.

I keep meaning to take in a lower league match, to cleanse myself of the Premier League "matchday" experience. Standing up, drinking in sight of the pitch, an experience frozen in time, considering the age and state of some of the grounds. The problem is, I never seem to get round to going, because following a football club already takes up so much of my spare time. Adding more football into the mix could be a step too far. Instead, I watch some non-City games on TV. Don't have to move to do that.

I enjoy this escape. A big match that does not involve City – in that they are not involved, and the result will not impinge on the success of their season. I get to enjoy football without the stress, but there still has to be an angle.

I wonder if it is possible to enjoy football this way all the time, to love the sport without having any team to follow? I guess many do that in a roundabout way, because many supporters of lower league teams will avidly watch Premier League football.

Can you really be passionate about football without a team? Football is more fun, it is more visceral, more important, more everything, when you have a vested interest. Any match takes on extra allure when you prefer one of the teams over the other. I am passionate about football, it consumes me, and yet ask me to watch a match where I have no strong opinions on the team or the outcome, and I will lose interest within ten minutes. Yes, a 30-yard volley into the top corner is always great to witness, but what are the consequences of the goal? There has to be a consequence. Or a bet resting on the match. Which is partly why gambling is so dangerous.

On this occasion, I watch Arsenal v Tottenham Hotspur, and choose well, Arsenal winning an amazing match 5-2. I hate both teams equally, again for spurious reasons, but it is impossible not to enjoy this match. Sometimes football is so good it can excite you even if you don't have that vested interest. But if having a preference does help, perhaps it helps explain tribalism and why we find it so easy to turn against players and teams.

Kitted Out

People are getting in a tizzy on Twitter due to City's kit for next season being leaked. It's not great, but I don't really care. I'd like a return to traditional designs and colours, but I'm not paying the ridiculous prices asked for such flimsy pieces of cotton anyway. Clubs get paid huge amounts of money by corporations who spit out templated kits season after season. We all know any fan with Photoshop skills could sit at a computer and do a better job, producing something that harks back to the club's history and traditions. It is what it is. Only the colour of the home kit is sacrosanct, which doesn't tally with one of my favourite kits - City's Kappa home kit in the 1990s, which was apparently laser blue, a made-up colour.

The debate online does get me a tad nostalgic though, and I delve into the deep recesses of my wardrobe, as I used to buy kits semi-regularly. There are some nice tops that I no longer fit into, and some abominations, usually an away kit. Webbing, brown sections, sashes and collars that vary in quality. I don't get worked up about the quality of City's kits, but there is something quite special in looking at any of them. Every past kit brings back memories – and I don't know if I am alone in this, but every kit conjures up the image of one player over all others.

Put your Phone Down, Colin

Bloody Twitter. I'm sat in a pub, as friends chat about beer, and I'm on the internet arguing with a faceless United fan. Is this really the best use of my time?

I understand Twitter fully now – it's funny, informative, addictive, and dangerous. A mine of information, and disinformation too. It appears to be dominated by a minority desperate for attention, probably because they see potential earnings as the natural consequence of a visible Twitter presence. They are the new breed of football "fan" emerging, created by the world wide web. I'm not sure they really like football, it is simply a vehicle for them to gain followers on the internet. And you don't gain attention on the internet with a series of calm, sensible opinions. It's so much easier to get worked up going through my Twitter feed than it is sat taking to anyone in real life, and I worry where this is leading. Some people live their lives online. I must try not to get drawn into every argument I see, as it serves no purpose. No one is winning here.

A good example popped up on my timeline just last week. There was an ongoing debate about the merits of Edin Dzeko. I saw some great points made, and some bad ones. But then it all got side-tracked, when a couple of anonymous posters made allegations that Dzeko gets a rougher ride than others solely because he is a Muslim. Soon the discussion collapsed into a thread of abuse and accusations. Any rational debate was over.

And it seems clear to me that the problem with social media is two-fold, away from its many good points. Firstly, some people feel the need to have an opinion about everything, despite clearly being an expert in absolutely nothing. Secondly, social media allows people to regularly project to the world what they are thinking. But telling the world what you think is rarely a good idea. If everything we thought was made public, we'd all be friendless.

I'm being overly harsh, focusing on the negative. Twitter is already helping me make connections with people I would otherwise have never known existed. Every day it makes me laugh out loud, and amazes me with people's humour and ingenuity. It is often at its best not when City win, but when United lose. But we tend as a species to focus on the bad stuff, and that's what stands out.

Anyway, I must now go. Time to rubberneck on Twitter once more, and feel worse for it. Scroll, scroll, scroll. Rinse and repeat.

Back On The Pitch

Great news. Carlos Tevez is officially back from exile, as City defeat Chelsea 2-1 in a must-win game. He was actually back weeks before, but this was the first time he makes it onto the pitch. The players say all the right things, about being glad he is back, and most City fans are glad too. He may not deserve another chance, but if it helps City, then it's all good. That's how it works. This time he does not refuse to come off the bench, and sets up a late winner for Samir Nasri. City's title hopes are alive, and I have aged quicker than time. Chelsea undeservedly took the lead in the 2nd half, and at that point it felt like the season was petering out. It was nice to see heads stay up, and the resolve to get the result.

When Tevez joined City, City's marketing people decided to have some fun. I say decided, some did, as not everyone was on board. I know someone at the club, and those who make such decisions were divided on whether to go ahead with a certain billboard suggested by a PR client. Plenty of staff at City did not take much pleasure over the billboard, as poking fun at United, however innocently, was not how they wanted the club run. Nevertheless, it was agreed to publish it, and soon after a "Welcome To Manchester" billboard appeared at the end of Deansgate, with Tevez on it.

This turned out to a be a marketing masterstroke. It played on the trope that United do not play their home games in Manchester, as Old Trafford is located in one of the ten boroughs of Greater Manchester, but not in the City of Manchester borough itself. Thus, even though Tevez had spent two years at United, by joining City he would play for a Manchester team for the first time. It worked so well mostly because so many failed to get the joke, and would fail to do so long after the event.

What was done was done. It went down a storm with City fans, and as for Tevez, he seemed fine with it. That's the thing with him - he doesn't seem to care much about getting on the wrong side of people, and he certainly doesn't seem to hold much affection for his previous club, or its manager. Such an attitude makes it easier to understand why we're willing to forgive and forget now he is back.

Moments Of Clarity

"How did City do?"

"Won 2-1 dad, played well."

"That's good. Are we top yet?"

"No, 2nd. But one win away from top, so it's going ok."

"I want to see us win the league again. One more time."

"I know, hopefully we won't have long to wait. We've waited a long time."

"That Sergio is a star. It says that in the newspaper."

"He's amazing. If he stays fit, we've got a great chance. A great chance."

"I was at Newcastle, you know?"

"We haven't played them away dad, so I don't think so."

"No, in 68. When we won the league."

"Oh. Wow. You remember?"

"Of course, why wouldn't I? Me and my friend Billie got one of the coaches. 4-3, Neil Young was unplayable. It was electric. What a side that was, son. The home fans clapped our goals, different times they were."

"It must have been amazing."

"Yes, it was. Me and Billie ran on the pitch at the end. All very good natured. They played "Congratulations" over the tannoy too, which was nice. Let's hope you get to feel that way soon, eh son?"

"Let's hope so."

"Maybe you'll run onto the pitch too."

"Not from the 2nd tier dad, not from the 2nd tier."

That day, dad can't stop talking about the 1968 title triumph, and I want to sit by his side forever. He calls the trip to Newcastle one of the best days of his life, after marrying mum, the birth of his three children, and the day he got Sky Plus. His little joke, I think.

Everything has changed since then, everything. Mum died in 2008. It was cancer that got her in the end, at the third attempt. My dad was never the same, but I felt a release when her suffering ended. Fifty-five years together, and I never heard them have a single argument. She wore the trousers in the relationship, and he knew when to say nothing and accept defeat. She spent decades worrying about my dad, especially his health. He enjoys life too much I remember her saying to me once as I dried the pots.

Dad never talks about mum anymore. I think he finds it too hard.

My mum, one she had mastered her basic Nokia phone, used to send me a text message that simply said "well done xx" when City won a game.

When City won their final game of the 2007/08 season against Portsmouth, before the season really tailed off. Mum was already very ill, and everyone knew she couldn't fight much longer. When I got the text message, it hit me hard knowing any message I got now could be her last.

I still have it on my phone.

My mum died with something of a broken heart, as my sisters and I failed to provide her with a grandchild. She never said as much, but then she didn't have to. She was always proud of anything we did, but I know there was something within her that craved the family line to continue, that wanted the grandma experience. Thanks to my sister, the line is saved, but too late for my mum to experience. Claire didn't like children, and I didn't like responsibility. It is what it is.

City won their first game the following season in the UEFA Cup, and soon after the full-time whistle went, I dug my phone out of my pocket, out of habit more than anything, and then I remembered.

I appreciated the messages, but I never replied to them, and I so wish I had.

Psyche

Before the match, we spend a few hours in our usual pub. There is grumbling because there are not as many beers on as usual. As is often the case, a friend brings a friend, a new face in the group, if only for one day. Graham is a psychiatrist, and apparently not that big a football fan, but there was a spare ticket so he fancied seeing what this football lark is all about. He reminded me of one of Phoebe's brief boyfriends on Friends, the shortest of relationships because he would use his powers for evil, exposing the group's insecurities, resulting in them despising him. Graham is not evil, and great company, but I can sense him analysing us all. Wondering what it is that makes us follow this routine every single week. He probably thinks we're a cult, and I would not argue if that were the case.

There is an interesting chat about why there is so much angst in the psyche of a football fan, even if things on the surface seem to be going quite well. I mentioned that I think I've worked out why it may feel like following a good team is not always that enjoyable, apart from the stress of competing for trophies on multiple fronts. And it's the probability that the elation of a win has a shorter shelf life than the low-level depression that follows a loss. We tend to dwell on the bad stuff rather than embrace the good stuff.

Graham corrects me on the depression comment, and I feel guilty for its use. He says he's read a few studies on this, and it fascinates him due to the blatant irrationality of football fans. He told us about the studies, and ticked off all our idiosyncrasies. Being a football fan is addictive, though I maintain that many continue to go to football matches because once you start it becomes self-fulfilling, and you just keep doing it for no deep reason, apart from escaping life. The addiction, the studies show is due to the fan trying to recreate that first high that football gave them. Younger fans are more energetic about their support, as with old age comes cynicism. Or maybe everything hurts when you get old, and you just want to sit down. The lure of watching sport is needing to know how the story ends, the pull of belonging, being part of a tribe, returning us to our primeval urges. It is more satisfying to celebrate a good result as a group, and perhaps it is more cathartic to mourn a bad result collectively. I fear that social media is breaking those norms though, if my Twitter feed is anything to go by. There is an element of schadenfreude too, which is why rivalries are so important. There is almost as much pleasure to be taken from the misfortune of a hated rival than the success of your own team. Almost.

"The problem with football fans is that their reactions are irrational. If your team has five terrible seasons and five great seasons, you should be cherishing the great ones, and forgetting the terrible ones. That's how you get the most out of life. Shit happens in life, but there's usually better times around the corner. My round, is it?"

Must-Win

Ah, must-win games. One of those phrases that is criminally overused in football. The win over Chelsea was not a must-win game. If City go on to win the league, there may be defining moments within its 90 minutes or so. Coming off the back of a defeat at Swansea, City would have been up against it if they had squandered more points. The momentum would have been with United, and the league title would very much have been in their hands. But with nine games to go, must-win it was not. Especially as City still have United to play.

However, that late Nasri goal may turn out to be a defining moment. One of those moments that changes the mood, and can alter the perception of a title race. From one point in two games, to three points in two games, but including a win over Chelsea, one of the pre-season favourites for the title. A late winner can also have restorative powers no medicine can match.

At full-time, it feels so good. This is why we follow our team, over land and sea. For moments like this. And this is why a scrappy win over poor opposition secured with a late goal can leave me in a better mood than a comprehensive thrashing that most expected.

Spiralling

And then it all goes wrong, quickly. That's the thing about life at, or near the top. When a team is involved in a relegation fight, every win can be vital. At the other end of the table, every defeat can be fatal. It only takes a fortnight or less for things to potentially unravel. City draw at Stoke, a game defined by two wonder strikes, one slightly deflected long-range shot from Yaya Toure and earlier a goal of the season contender from Peter Crouch, another man with surprisingly good feet for a big man. I tell everyone that will listen that he committed a foul before lobbing the ball in from 40 yards, but no one wants to ruin the special moment. Then it gets worse. City need a late equaliser to grab a draw at home to Sunderland. This leaves me conflicted, as how should I feel about a late equaliser in a game City should win comfortably? Not all late goals are equal, it seems. There is worse to come. A late Mikel Arteta goal sees City lose at Arsenal. To make matters even worse than that, Mario Balotelli is once more a headline-grabber, sent off for two yellow cards.

Six months of progress wiped out in a fortnight. City are eight points behind United in the table, and with this defeat, it feels like it is all over. It was not to be, my dreams lying wrecked on the shore. Amazingly, as the end of all this, I feel a certain calm. City's title campaign has faded away, my hope of seeing my captain lift the league trophy looks to have gone. But it a release for me to see City fade away. The tension, the stress, it has largely evaporated. The air of disappointment seems quite pleasant in comparison. Maybe I am kidding myself, but United won't let it slip from here, and with City out of all other competitions, the importance of the coming games has subsided.

I walk towards the tram with Dave. That was shit, and the league is gone is the only football chat we engage in. There is much silence, replicated in the mood outside the ground. People rush to get away, and the less said, the better. What is there to say? Now is not the time to lay into individual players, discuss Mancini's tactics or whether certain players should be dropped. Another time. This is the time for getting home, trying to get sleep, and forgetting for now that your football team has just messed up the first top-level title challenge of your lifetime.

Where does this leave the club? Have they overachieved, or underachieved? Were they really title contenders? As always, every opinion is available online. What's more, are City officially in crisis? It doesn't take much for the English media to designate such a status to a club. A couple of defeats can be enough, and soon a cracked club crest will appear on the back page of the Sun newspaper. Despite the stress easing off, I am desperately disappointed. But sensible enough, I hope, to understand that it wasn't to be, City are in a great place right now, and the future is bright. It's no surprise that a post mortem is carried out on the team. There is a strange culture in the UK where celebrating the victors is almost a side-issue to piling in on the losers.

Ultimately, if at the end of a season you look back and the worst team you've seen at your ground is your own team, then you've got grounds for complaint. As my uncle once told me after a particularly incompetent City performance, "worse things happens at sea". I've no idea what horrific things are happening at sea, and his comment wasn't of great comfort, truth be told. But yeah, could be worse.

If I have learned one thing, it is that tight title races are mentally draining. Exhausting. Perhaps more so than relegation fights, as there is so little room for error. Does it get any easier? Are United fans feeling the same stress as they go for yet another title? I'm not sure I can cope with another five years of this, let alone thirty.

"Real" Football

In the end, I do get to go to a lower league football match.

I am in Rochdale for a day, to attend a mindfulness course, which management make quite clear is compulsory, hosted by a life coach with very big muscles. The day includes health checks, and Greg, a man I am soon wishing a thousand painful deaths on, tells me I am 6 foot tall, but would be two inches taller if I didn't slouch all the time. As I wasn't slouching at the time my height was measured, I'm not sure he is such an expert on the human body after all. And when you've witnessed five relegations, you're bound to slouch occasionally.

The day is unfulfilling and pointless, and I leave the grey concrete slab-like office block feeling worse than when I entered, though also relieved that a day of telling me to focus, believe and strategize my future is now over, for at least another year. My cousin, a season ticket holder at Rochdale suggests I come along to watch his team that night, as they are at home to Tranmere Rovers and I am in the area. I will stay over at his and have the next day off, perhaps take in a film by myself.

And so off to Spotland I go. The ground has been around since 1878, and you can tell. It is a basic ground, but like any arena it is special to its occupants, the holder of so many memories and special nights. Memories in every pore of its structure, and the buzz of a new ground.

How many special nights it has hosted, I am not sure. I like to keep abreast of the results of all the local teams, by which I mean those in the general vicinity of Manchester – Oldham Athletic, Bury, Rochdale. Stockport County, Bolton Wanderers and even Wigan Athletic at a push. I want them to do well, Stockport excepted, because I have no grudges to bear.

I always perceive Rochdale as a club that have eternally treaded water, thus giving their supporters quite a banal existence. That's not a dig, it's just I feel they rarely get promoted, rarely get relegated, but just "exist".

Well not anymore – the 2009/109 season saw the end of a 41 year wait for promotion, though this year relegation is a real possibility. Even more so after this match, a dour affair that Rochdale lose 2-0.

And yeah, I enjoyed my evening under the lights. There was a freedom to it all, from getting into the ground, to being able to drink a pint where I wanted, to witnessing football on a pitch that could surprise the most talented of players. Even stood up. I got a delicious meat and potato pie at half time that scalded my mouth, and some cooking lager to wash it down. Different smells, a different atmosphere, and somehow even colder than any Etihad night match. The crowd were quite forgiving too, considering the awful fayre on show. The angst of needing to succeed at all costs seemed absent. At least once a season, I must do this again.

My cousin is called Terry, and once we are back at his place, he is fairly quiet, the default setting for a football fan after a disappointing performance. It will be such a shame, he says. What will, I ask.

He explains. After more than 40 years, to go up and then not consolidate and strengthen, or even spend 40 years in this new division instead, would be a shame. To go back down so soon, after just two seasons, especially after surviving the promotion season, would be a kick in the guts. I cannot disagree.

To add a later note, I should inform you that the 2011/12 season did indeed result in a kick in the guts for Terry and all Rochdale fans.

The next day, I am one of eight people to witness the 2pm showing of Hunger Games. I recommend it.

Fair Enough

Back to City's struggles.

Football fans have numerous coping mechanisms for dealing with failure, and even more for dealing with the success of others. For the latter, the most common mechanism is to underplay the success, and add an asterisk to any achievements. The team cheated, got all the refereeing decisions, bought the title, were lucky with injuries (unlike my team!) and so on. Their success doesn't count, basically. As a final resort you can simply state that you don't care, or invoke some nostalgia, bemoaning how football isn't what it used to be, and telling anyone who will listen that you are falling out of love with football, coincidentally at precisely the same time that your team has become less successful.

I type out a long diatribe on Facebook in a weaker moment, then delete it, because it is rather pitiful and who wins if I end up arguing on the internet about football? More to the point, if United go on to win the league, they deserve it. No point being petty about it, and not one of their fans will spend a single second wondering how rival fans rate the achievement.

By the end of this book, you will come to the conclusion that I have no coping mechanisms at all for dealing with the stresses of fandom. There is only one way to get over a bad result though, or the success of other teams – and that is time. It does heal, and football is cyclical so there's always another game, another season, another talking point to concentrate on before long.

Robot Wars

As football fans, what do we want and expect from our players? Robots, who are consistent and rarely falter? Players we know very little about, because they are consummate professionals? Or mavericks, who may let you down, but can at any moment do something amazing, and it will be one hell of a ride along the way? Or a mixture of the two? We expect footballers to be metronomes, but who knows what is going on in their life? Who knows how much they truly care about their job? Does the wage they receive mean they must be devoted to the cause, or can they hate their lot as much as I do?

So many questions.

I may be in the minority, but I err towards wanting robots. I have got the taste for success, at long last, and I want my team to win every game, and that's the most important thing to me. There's always room for the odd maverick, but they cannot be allowed to affect the equilibrium. Maybe it's sad that I place success over everything else, but I am merely the product of modern football. Where there is little nuance, and everything must be the best or the worst. Where you are either a genius or a fraud. And with City, where there is an absolute demand for constant success now due to the investment in the side and the club as a whole.

I feel for Mario Balotelli, the reason I am saying all this. He is clearly a nice guy. He attracts trouble, and sometimes it is clear many, including match officials, have it in for him. But he created this storm before it became an unstoppable force. Now it seems it is self-fulfilling. Stereotypes are often exaggerated and unfair, but they all have a root in at least a kernel of truth. There is an industry of its own dealing with stories about Mario away from the pitch, most of them false. The bottom line though is that he just doesn't seem to have the psyche to be a consistent, top-level performer, despite having the skillset to do so. Years down the line, what will his legacy be? He could be a Ballon D'Or winner, if only he wanted to.

I could write a book on him, a fascinating man. I feel conflicted when I talk about him, but right now I am at the end of my tether. My confidence in him has eroded, after one incident too many. Non-league football is littered with players who had all the skill, but never applied it to maximum effect. With Mario Balotelli, you never know what you are going to get. But with a player of his undoubted ability, you should know what you're getting.

It is Mario's character that makes him a favourite amongst City fans, but how much leeway can we give him? And why should he get different treatment to any other player? There is an uncertainty in how to judge him because it feels like we are at a point where he would get sent off even when he does nothing wrong. His reputation was clearly based on some truth, but now it damns him whatever he does. He is a marked man with referees, and it seems like he can't win right now. Other players get away with far more than he ever will. I hope he turns it around, as his ceiling is as high as anyone else in the squad. But I just can't see him consistently hitting the highest notes.

Who Am I?

I'm the coward who won't go to Old Trafford, and is now already dreading the return fixture when the away support will be gloating like never before.

You can split football fans into three distinct groups: the optimists, the pessimists and those that maintain a balance, and some may say, have a greater grip on reality. I'm firmly in the pessimist camp. But hey, if you expect everything to go wrong, you're rarely disappointed. This pessimism best illustrates itself, as I am now discovering, when you peruse the fixture list of a title rival. To a pessimist, your rivals have an easy fixture list, and they seem certain to win every game. On the flip side, your team has some really tough games to come, and dropped points seem inevitable. I'm not sure how many trophies my team needs to win for me to shake off this pessimism. Maybe there is no magic number, and this is how life will always be. It is why I can never relax in a game unless City are four goals up. Three goals if there is under ten minutes left. Two goals if the game is into injury time.

Truth is, it's not pessimism as such. That would imply I expect my club to lose every game, and I do not. They are really good at this football lark, after all. What it really is, is nerves. I am a nervous supporter, and this can sometimes be interpretated as negativity. It's a fine line.

There are kids who have just started supporting City, who will grow up with a completely different psyche to me, should the club be regularly successful in the future, as seems likely. They certainly shouldn't be involved in many relegation fights, that much is clear. And for a fan growing up knowing only success, watching the likes of David Silva and Sergio Aguero from day one, they will never know my pessimism, and will be so much better off because of that. To quote my friend's saying: "they don't know they're born".

Moving On

There's time for a quick pint or two after the Arsenal match, and the discussion turns to what sort of loss stays with you the longest. A team underperforming, the manager getting his tactics wrong, or losing due to bad luck or a refereeing *disasterclass*. While I think referees can be subject to far too much criticism, it is the last option that I plump for, though I am alone in the group in feeling this way. I can accept that my team may play badly sometimes, and that individuals can have a nightmare 90 minutes. But an injustice that affects a result lingers like a bad smell. The league table never lies, apparently, but feeling cheated after a game makes me think otherwise. When a result is not fair, in my eyes, that's the worst.

The defeat at Arsenal hits me badly, as expected, before the fog lifts a day or so later when I realise that there is nothing to fear now. Naturally there is talk of whether this squad is as good as we thought. Edin Dzeko is a player I love, but he has been in indifferent form much of the season. He sparkles in bursts. When you add into the mix the enigma that is Mario Balotelli, and the fact Carlos Tevez was thousands of miles away for much of the season, it seems the squad was not so top heavy in attack after all. It's still a wonderful squad. The slump in form has allowed the tradition of criticising full-backs to resume. Gael Clichy was one of the summer signings, a steady hand, who lacks the explosiveness of Aleksandar Kolarov, whose form is unfortunately erratic. Clone half of each and you'd have something quite special.

I'm ok. I needed football to save me, and for a while it did. But ultimately I need to save myself. Life is acceptable, and I support a wonderful football team, have a wonderful group of friends who are a support network without realising it, and today I saw my dad and he laughed until tears formed at an old anecdote about him and his friends and what they used to get up to. He looks so frail now, but I am looking for positives where I can find them. My team is on the up, even if it doesn't feel like it right now.

Dad has some of his belongings in a storage unit in Cheetham Hill, gathering dust. One evening, bored with watching repeats of The Wire, I drive over and look through his old City newspaper clippings that he keeps in five different scrapbooks. The photos of the crowds beguile me more than anything. I sit there for two hours, reading, learning, shed a few tears and not once do I look at my phone.

On The Road

I am excited. I am going to an away game, a long way away. Well, Norwich, but it seems like a long way away, considering they haven't discovered the joys of motorways yet. It no longer feels like a must-win game, because three points probably doesn't matter anymore, allowing me to enjoy the trip without consequences.

OK, maybe there is just a hint of expectation. Midweek, City got back to winning ways, by beating West Bromwich Albion 4-0. At the same time, United fell to a shock 1-0 defeat to Wigan Athletic. Another match where I constantly glance at my phone, on this occasion awaiting the confirmation of the inevitable United equaliser and then winner, neither of which ever arrive. So the gap is down to five points again. I am in a better mood, but United will be focused now. I don't see it making much difference, and the games are running out.

It's an early start, as it's an early kick off. By 10:30am, we have reached the designated pub, and have time for a few pre-match pints as we put on our football and Grand National bets. Then on to Carrow Road, a new ground for me, which adds to the occasion.

For the 2nd time this season, City win 1-6 away from home. And like the Old Trafford massacre, the score line does not tell an accurate story of how the match went. In fact, the two games have many parallels. City went two goals up pretty early, but Norwich peg the visitors back soon after half-time. It takes another late flurry of goals, in the last 15 minutes, to see City home with ease.

After one of his goals, Carlos Tevez, scorer of a hat-trick on the day, celebrates with a golf swing in front of the City fans. This is in reference to Roberto Mancini's barbed reference to him playing golf in Argentina for the past five months. City fans lap it up.

Perhaps we shouldn't, but we do. It's easy for a footballer to win over a fan base after a discretion. Just score an important goal, make an important block, perhaps kiss the badge too. Basically, just be good at football, and all is forgiven. We have short memories, when it suits. And very long memories, when considering other football clubs' indiscretions. I still bear a grudge for a bad tackle made in a game in 2002. I will take that grudge with me to the grave.

Job done, and a fun ninety minutes. I like the ground, and the pleasant atmosphere outside. Back to the pub, more drinks, torn up betting slips and a heavy night, one of those where not everyone is accounted for by the end of the night, but everyone is there for the drive back the following day. During that drive, Manchester United beat Aston Villa 4-0, keeping their lead at the top to five points. I expected no favours from Aston Villa, and that's precisely what I got.

It's a long journey, and I am back on my phone. I notice someone saying that City just need to concentrate on their own results. I see this a lot, and it seems to ignore the way league tables operate. But whatever the truth, it feels clear to me now that Roberto Mancini and the players will probably be thinking that way. Thinking that they just do their own thing, and see where it takes them. Drop any points now, and it feels like it would be 100% over.

The Tides Of Change

A lot of the football crowd are at a birthday do one Friday night, hovering near the unopened buffet, as our stomachs need lining. I spot some mushroom vol au vents and feel a wave of nostalgia. Weddings, my gran's 70th birthday party at the cricket club, the odd funeral where I had to be on my best behaviour. My childhood and youth was full of these "spreads", and the odour of egg sandwiches and halved pork pies.

A couple of my mates are once more talking about not renewing their season ticket. Prices are rising again, as they always do. But that is not the reason, as some just aren't getting the buzz anymore, at the worst possible time. They will almost certainly renew, but this is an opportunity for them to vent. I will – I have no other way to fil my days.

I feel that change is coming, not just among my friends. Everything is. I think I fear it too. A world where young fans support players not teams (as is their right, I guess). Where money rules all facets of the game. A sport controlled and fought over by billionaires, that resembles politics more and more with each passing year. Should all this affect my ability to enjoy a match at The Etihad? Possibly not, but its effects creep over you, into every aspect of the sport.

What do I want different? Football was always supposed to be for the masses, a working-class game. Ticket prices need to be much cheaper. Anyone should be able to go to a match. They should be able to stand at a match too, if that's their preference.

Ultimately, it feels like we are moaning for the sake of it. We don't want to stand at matches anymore. The football is great. We can afford our season tickets. There's so much to enjoy.

One advantage of supporting a team who are now a contender for trophies, is that the games mean something. Not all games match these criteria. There are many fans who go to football matches week-in, week-out merely out of a sense of duty. The whole experience is a chore, but one that they feel duty-bound to fulfil. When my team was involved in one of its many relegation fights, I often wished to be a supporter of a mid-table side, as it would be much less stressful. And now I am supporting a team that is in a title race – just – maybe? - I am once more having similar thoughts, though with less conviction this time around. Why am I always looking towards that middle ground? Because as always, I want an easy life. You don't get to choose that life as a football fan though. It is chosen for you. Hence why that defeat at Arsenal gave me a sense of release.

.

Football Takes Years Off You

As fans are we too angry? I have just watched a European game, and there was an away fan celebrating in the home end, and no one around him seem remotely bothered. Do that in an English ground, and you'd be eating hospital food for a month. Truth is, I have no desire to sit with opposition fans, I can think of little worse. Results do matter to fans, and having someone celebrate your bad news by your side is not my idea of fun. However, there's probably not many sports in the world where rival supporters cannot mingle.

We are angry, there's no denying that. But some live for being angry. Some live for the confrontation, such as those whose ideal seat is next to the opposition fans, who spend most of a match looking away from the action, because goading fellow human beings is preferable to supporting their team. If you get very angry about football, I'd wager we're getting a mirror into the rest of your life.

The stress that football fans get themselves into is no laughing matter much of the time. The state we get ourselves in can have serious consequences. I've heard about too many fans having heart attacks during and after matches. How many have reduced live expectancies from the stress they censure? Studies have even showed that fans eat unhealthier after bad results. Domestic violence rates rocket after a bad result for a national side. There is even evidence of reckless driving increasing after defeats.

Define Me

I have decided to write a piece for the fanzine, and go for a theme that lingered in my brain recently when discussing key games in my upbringing over a post-match pint and burger so tall I had to cut it in half. The theme was games that define me as a City fan, and if they exist. Are there matches that sum up my journey? It seemed worthy of an article, as the actual football would be covered by many other writers in the next issue.

You are shaped by your team. Or maybe your team shapes you, picks you. Line up a hundred City and United fans in front of me, in plain clothing, and I reckon I could tell you which team they supported with at least an 80% accuracy rate. We just look different, often in a subtle way, though the obvious retort is to suggest that the haggard ones are the City fans. I hope that joke becomes less relevant in future.

I think there are matches that define you, and the nature of the game changes as the club changes. Maybe I change with it. The early games deal with failure and misery. Two games I have already mentioned definitely shaped me. Being relegated by losing at home to Luton in 1983, one of my first memories. Relegation in 1996, when City played for a draw against Liverpool despite needing to win. If anything summed up the ineptness of my football club, that was it. It wasn't all bad. With relegations came promotions. The play-off victory in 1999 defined me, as it was a reminder of what my club meant to me, and what joy they could give me, even at their lowest ebbs. The final game at Maine Road felt like a perfect allegory for the club I then supported, and my experiences. A new stadium, new hope, and a club that seemed at least to be on the up. And yet they lost that final game 1-0 at home to Southampton, and I filled away from the ground for the final time with an emptiness inside me. This was my life. Glimmers of a brighter future, but ultimately reality would bring me back down to earth. I could not possibly have imagined what may ahead.

So if one game in recent times defines me and my club, it is the semi-final win over United in the FA Cup. A game that confirmed one thing. The club and team I support is different now. Different quality, different expectations, and for the fans, there must now be a different mentality. No more underdog, no more expecting the worst. Believe. And with it must come a level of arrogance. I'm not sure you avoid that entirely if your team is successful.

One Last Time

It was around the time that my dad misplaced his car that I realised there was a rapidly shrinking window to do something I had intended to do for years - go to a match with my dad again. So before it was too late, that is what we did. On 19th December 2009, I took my dad to watch City v Sunderland. We sat in the posh seats, near the half-way line. It was cold, so we wrapped up warm. We were lucky, as City won a classic, 4-3, with Roque Santa Cruz scoring two goals, a rarity. My dad seemed to enjoy himself, though the thought persisted that I was doing this for me, and not him. We got a pint at half-time, and talked about the great sides of the past. He told me he didn't like the Etihad, and City should never have moved from Maine Road. On the way back from the match, we stopped near home, and I bought us both chips and gravy, and a can of fizzy Vimto. My treat. We ate our food in the car with wooden forks, as rain bounced off the windows, listening to the football reports. The drink gave him indigestion.

"Best not tell mum we've had this," dad joked.

He remembered.

Sunday, 22nd April 2012.

I write this with palpitations, and laboured breathing. I am not sure I can take much more of this, and thankfully I won't have to.

This was a day where the stress came with a double dose, but it was a day that may alter the history of Manchester City.

United are five points clear of City, and are playing on the same day, but not at the same time. United play at home to Everton, then City play at Wolves. I expect United to win, as always, so my expectations are low, and my stress levels fluctuate wildly by the minute. I'm still on edge, because, well, you know – the usual reasons.

As United are playing first, the pubs are bound to be full of their fans, so a few of us decide to watch the match at my place. I put the United match on, and when they go 3-1 up, we decamp to the local pub, safe in the knowledge that Everton are not going to do us any favours. Add them to the list, again. In the pub, the goals flow, and it is soon 4-2. Then 4-3. Then astonishingly it is 4-4. Steven Pienaar scores the equaliser, and lifts his shirt to reveal the message "God Is Great". If God has had any input in producing this score, I will renounce atheism immediately. The game is not on where we are, I have only the internet as my guide. But we all know, that if United drop two points, then suddenly City have a chance, as the Manchester Derby looms on the horizon.

Surely not?

I feel so sick.

With five minutes of the match to go, everyone else goes outside for a cigarette. I don't smoke, and can't move anyway. I consider starting smoking. Can I do that for ten minutes, then give up? No, of course not. But alcohol alone is not helping me right now. I start biting my fingers, pure anxiety overwhelming me. I sit in the pub alone, my heart beating through my chest, waiting for the inevitable United winner. I know how this plays out. False hope, one of the worst aspects of being a football fan. Sometimes it is better to have no hope at all. I refresh the live scores website I am staring at, as time drags slower than ever. Pure torture, second by second by second.

United are going to score.

Or so I thought. They do not score. The game ends 4-4, and United move six points ahead of City, having played a game more. This changes everything – if City can beat Wolves.

The mood is transformed. Giddiness, nerves, anticipation, more nerves. Don't fuck up this opportunity City. I run out of the pub and tell everyone. They don't believe me, for a few seconds at least. I wouldn't joke about this.

City don't fuck it up. Against a struggling Wolves side, goals from Sergio Aguero in the first half and Samir Nasri to calm the nerves in the second half ensures City close the gap to three points, with a superior goal difference. Everything now points towards one game, where there would be so much at stake that I try to blank it from my mind. But it's too late for that, for it is too big to ignore. This is going to the wire. And so as the full-time whistle is greeted with torrential rain, I remind myself that there is just three games to go. And next up would be the battle between the top two. It's going to be a long and unproductive week. The media coverage will saturate every area of my life. Ex-United players will be wheeled out to discuss how United will have an advantage, as they have been here before, many times. Sky's marketing department will be putting on long shifts creating montages to push the game. I don't know how I will cope with this week. And that's why the game is actually the easy bit. It's the build-up, the waiting that is unbearable.

City's win means Wolves are relegated. Their caretaker manager Terry Connor, a club legend, a man who bleeds gold, is in tears after the match. I always feel a sense of guilt on the rare occasion that City relegate another team, even if I don't like them very much, and I have nothing against Wolves. Someone has to go down and someone has to strike the final blow, but I know from bitter experience what it feels like. The writing was on the wall for Wolves though, and if it hadn't happened today, it would have happened soon. Nevertheless, the moment it is confirmed is a truly terrible moment. Despair and emptiness, followed by the inevitable recriminations. For me the worst bit was always wondering whether the club's best players were now destined to move on. That hurt more than anything, saying goodbye.

I don't harbour a desire for Wolves to go down, and even if I did, I'd have some sympathy for their fans on a day like this. Seeing your team get relegated is brutal, worse surely than if my team fail in their title challenge this, or any other season. I've seen my team get relegated five times, though as they are currently in the same division as when I first started supporting them, the plus side is I have seen my team promoted five times too. I've danced on the pitch, and drunk late into the night with the hope that things were now going to get better.

The relegations though, they stay in the mind even more. I've mentioned them some of them before – told you they stay in the mind. They were part of me, but with each passing year, they become more and more a part of a past life that I no longer associate with. The first time as you know was 1983, and I was a mere seven years old. City lost 1-0 at home to fellow relegation candidates Luton Town after a late goal, and David Pleat danced across the Maine Road turf to embrace his captain Brian Horton, who would later manage City. Naturally I've hated Pleat ever since.

I remember sitting in the kitchen listening to the game on the radio, but I don't remember my reaction. I imagine there were tears. There were plenty in my childhood as I was an emotional sort - a bruised knee after falling off my bike was usually enough to get me going.

1987 was the scene of the next relegation, and by now I was at an age where the impact of my team's failures was greater. It hit hard, but the three subsequent relegations hit even harder. 1996 saw the consequences of the Alan Ball reign, and it led to City's greatest ever fall from grace. Within two years, City had slid into the 3rd tier of English football for the first time in their history. City scored five goals and were relegated on the final day — typical.

There was one more relegation to endure, following on from two successive promotions, but after City returned to the top flight in 2002, they have remained there ever since. Money rules football, and my club has lots of it now. It seems hard for my psyche to accept that I will probably never see my team relegated again, but that is part and parcel of being a City fan right now. How I think about my team has to change. No more having our bellies tickled, or our lunchbox stolen in the playground. And whether we win a hundred trophies or none at all, I'm thankful for that.

The one thing you can say about City is that when not managed by Stuart Pearce, they were rarely boring. Incompetent perhaps, but never boring.

Mind Tricks

As an aside, in this modern world we all inhabit, I could not cope with enduring a big match via the medium of radio. Radio is wonderful, but it's not for big matches, as your mind runs amok. Every opposition attack feels like an impending goal, and it's hard for me to gauge the feel of the match off an audio feed. Radio works best for me on a longish car journey, when other teams are playing, and scores are coming in from across the country. Radio is for phone ins and reactions after your team has won. Or maybe it can feel cathartic listening to the inquest after a loss.

After City secure the points, we return to the pub for a nightcap. The mood is electric, and some are swaying when they walk. With a couple more drinks, we put the sport to rights, and I contradict myself about football not requiring changes by claiming penalty areas are too big and matches should be an hour long and counted down on a clock when the ball is in play. I stumble home with another meat feast pizza that leaves me full of regret the following morning, when I polish off the remaining third as my breakfast.

I always make it home, we all do, but sometimes I wonder how.

After Breakfast

The next day, I'm in a great mood, but I am still thinking about Wolves. There are images burned into my retinas, as Sky love to scan a crowd and pick out misery, especially if it involves a child crying. They show no mercy. And I am thinking about those shots – there but for the grace of God go I. And I try to think of the positives - In the aftermath of a relegation, there is a silver lining. Promotion pushes are infinitely more enjoyable than relegation battles. This may not be applicable to Wolves and their journey, but for a team that spends season after season with the sole objective of not getting relegated, is a season in the Championship, watching your team win more games and seeing your team higher up a table not ultimately a more enjoyable experience, week-on-week? I guess it's easy for me to say now that I don't have to worry about such things, but relegation fights have provided me with some of my most wretched periods as a football fan, and promotion seasons some of my most joyous. There is a caveat – I never want to experience the nerves of a play-off final penalty shoot-out ever again, thank you very much.

A big win gives fans a unique feeling. I have gone into such matches off the back of a crap week. Weeks when nothing goes right, the stress levels are off the chart and you feel like you are firefighting every second of every day. But after a big win, that can all be forgotten, if only for a day. Watching football has always been a form of escapism, and that's never truer when it allows you to forget everything else in the world. It's a special kind of contentment, knowing that today at least, the world has been kind to me.

How Many Hands?

"It's in City's hands now."

"Eh, is it?"

"Well yeah, of course. If City win their remaining games, they're champions."

"Yeah, but if United win their games, they are champions also. So it is surely in their hands too?"

"Well yeah, I guess so. We have to play them, but it's at home, so it's more in our hands."

"I'm sorry but no, it can't be in both teams' hands. Only one team can have destiny in their hands."

"Wait, what? Look, I've had plenty to drink, that much is true, but I stand by my point. City win their games, it's in the bag. In their hands."

"Yes, but it cannot be in the hands of two separate teams. Ownership of the title's destiny is singular."

"Eh? Yes it can. You know what? Never mind."

Derby Day

The back page of The Mirror calls the match bigger than the World Cup. I'm not sure how they decided that, but the game is huge, that much is clear. A title decider as Alex Ferguson called it after the Everton match.

Recently, Real Madrid and Barcelona played each other four times across three competitions within three weeks. I cannot comprehend how I would have dealt with that situation, and I hope I never have to. Even if City beat United four times in a few weeks, I am not sure the mental strain would make it worthwhile. OK, maybe just.

I don't need to tell you my state of mind for this game. Low appetite, distracted, nauseous. The oxymoron of the week dragging and one of the most important matches of my lifetime approaching on the horizon at considerable speed. Time is warped once more, perhaps because I can't think straight. Another Monday night match means that the wait becomes even more painful.

In January 2010, Manchester City's League Cup semi-final leg at home to United was called off because of snow. When I heard the news, I did a silent jig at the thought that the stress of Derby Day had been delayed. Yet this thought process made no sense. I had already gone through many of the stages of stress and anxiety leading up to the match, and now would have to go through the entire process again. Putting it off might feel good in the present, when the news arrives, but ultimately it just meant more stress than before. It's better to get these matches over with, however painful that may be.

The drag of another long week, overthinking the next game, secretly hoping that all United's best players pick up training ground injuries before the weekend. It is considered bad form to wish injury on a player, even if it means they miss a big game against your side, in a similar way that it's bad form to point out that your team have an excellent record against their next opponents, as this apparently is tempting fate. I am as superstitious as anyone, but I don't think I have god-level abilities to alter results with a single utterance, and nor does anyone else. I wish that were not the case. Alex Ferguson probably thinks he can as the anointed master of mind games, but he'd be wrong. I guess the compromise that avoids endless guilt is for an opponent's star player to pick up a minor injury that means he misses a single match, against your team. This allows him to help you further by being available when his team plays your rivals. Win/win.

D Day

I regret taking the day off work. I need to pass the time, but I cannot concentrate. I pick up a book, and read one line eight times before giving up. I turn the TV on. Two hundred channels, all rubbish. There's only one option left. I decide to clean the flat. I wash the pots. Wipe down some surfaces. Get the Toilet Duck out. Clean the shower head. Even the hoover gets an outing.

I reorganise the spice rack. Take some rubbish to the bins, plus some cardboard boxes and tins. I stare out the window for a while. Watch two squirrels frolicking and a wood pigeon making a right racket. Clean a window. Polish the TV and PlayStation. Look in the oven and remind myself it needs a clean, and promise myself that I will definitely do it soon. Walk around for a bit, for no particular reason. Delete some emails. Finally change the bulb in the hallway. Put two rolls of toilet paper in the bathroom. Clean the smear off two taps. Walk around a bit more. Stare out the window again.

I relent and look at the clock in the living room. Twenty minutes has passed. Twenty bloody minutes.

Fucking Derby Day.

Finally, time progresses, and there's no putting this one off. I arrive at the ground fairly sober, as I feel too ill to drink much. There are about fifteen of us in the pub, choosing one we know will not see any trouble. There's talk, but there is more silence than normal. And then the time arrives. Taxis, to the ground. Here we go.

The atmosphere is overpowering, and I cannot sit still. But at least the match is now happening.

A match that Manchester City win.

Tides Turn

I had little to worry about. Something important dawns on me close to the end of this match. The thing I thought would never happen in my lifetime, has happened. I am being a tad presumptuous here, as City may not win the league and my argument falls over at that point, but it is how it feels at this moment – City are better than United.

Alex Ferguson, with his line up, and his approach to the game, a game they cannot afford to lose, waved a white flag. The side is dour, defensive, tentative, and do not have a shot on target across the whole match. They are everything United have not been for decades, everything I have had to endure and ultimately respect for so long. They barely get near the City goal, and in a game my side must win, I am strangely calm. They are not a threat. The game is settled in an iconic moment, captain fantastic Vincent Kompany heading home a David Silva corner shortly before half-time. It is not a classic match, but that is irrelevant. City win, City are top of the league on goal difference, and there are just two league games to go. What's more, we, the fans, made a difference. The atmosphere carried the players home.

United may not get close to City's goal, but still I must deal with such a huge match, when one moment could change my mood, change everything. When my team are winning a tense, tough match, I try to ignore time. I try not to look at the clock, as it seems to slow down every occasion I take a glance. History's greatest scientific minds could not explain how time stands still when your team has a narrow lead late in a match.

Eventually you can't help but look. Damn. 72 minutes gone, thought we were close to 80 by now. Slowly, time moves. You know when injury time arrives, the board goes up. Then the clock is of no use, as it stops at the Etihad. Now you're counting down the seconds in your head.

Win a free kick! Take it into the corner!

A huge groan. Possession conceded. Idiot.

Roberto Mancini is arguing with Alex Ferguson on the touchline, and I love him even more.

Keep the ball! Win a free kick!

You're just waiting for that peep of the referee's whistle. The allocated injury time is up, and yet they play on. Bloody referee. Palpitations. To hear that sweet sound emanating from the referee's mouth.

And there it is. His arms raised. The relief is palpable. The roar of the crowd. Job done. It was a good day after all. It was the best day, the stuff of dreams.

The beauty of streaming out the ground after a result like that. I'm literally bouncing. This is beautiful, so beautiful.

Even after the match, I sit in a pub, and I cannot finish my pint. I'm still so wound up, tense and anxious that the euphoria of a victory cannot remove the nausea and the claustrophobia of this title run-in. I drain the remnants into a plant pot whilst no one is looking. I will not sleep well tonight, despite the day going perfectly. There will be a million thoughts racing through my head. Two cup finals left.

Am I even happy? Of course I am, but I am also exhausted. I know that the two weeks ahead will be no calmer.

Diversions

You want to gloat, you really do. City have done the double over their biggest rivals. They've gone top of the league. They win the last two games, and they are champions of England.

Champions of England.

But they have to win those last two games, against two very different opponents.

As any football fan knows, gloating can come back to haunt you, and the stakes are too high here. There is an uneasy truce in the office. My United-supporting friends have disappeared off Facebook, again. But I must bite my lip. Put my head down, try not to think about next weekend, do my work, and just survive. Now is not the time to be shouting from the rooftops.

The night before the Newcastle match, I decide to go to another comedy gig, which I hope will take my mind off football, if only for a couple of hours. To fill the void of "the night before the big match". Sadly, I replace the panic of a title race with the panic of sitting too close to the front for a comedian who it turns out loves to talk to the audience, having not prepared enough material of his own. Thankfully he does not decide to talk to me, reaching the couple next to me before stopping, but the stress levels are now off the chart. There is no escape, until the season is over. Resistance is futile.

As I get back from the gig, I get call from my friend Simon. His brother has got man flu, the worst type of flu. He is bed-ridden for the foreseeable future. Would I like a ticket to the Newcastle match?

My heart races once the question ends. My mind races too. There is a lot to take in here, and the first consideration is that I am the least impulsive person that has ever walked the earth. I like my week planned out, and to know what lies ahead. Suddenly I am offered the opportunity to travel to Newcastle to watch one of the most important football matches of my life. I have already arranged to watch the match with three friends in a local pub. I then feel guilt for some reason at the thought of bailing on them. And finally, of course, there is the age-old issue of my bravado. Or lack of it.

The answer is obvious, though. It's time to stop being a coward.

The Penultimate Game

The next morning, I'm on a local supporter group's coach, on my way to St James' Park. My first beer is at 8am, by which time many are on their 3rd drink at least. It is a 1:30pm kick off, so time really is of the essence. The coach has a toilet, but it resembles the one out of Trainspotting by 10am. A service station stop on the way is well appreciated.

As anyone who has been in the away end at Newcastle knows, the seats are in the gods. I am exhausted by the time I reach my seat, though I have sobered up considerably. But no amount of alcohol can mask my nerves, back at the ground where City last won the league.

The atmosphere is hard to describe. You can feel almost every emotion in the air. It crackles. There is an upbeat feel, but undoubtedly an air of tension too. Even the chants have an element of nervousness in them. The longer the game goes on, the more it envelops us all.

I may have been slightly more relaxed if Newcastle were on the beach by now, counting down the days until the end of the season. But this is a good side, who have everything to play for, having just won at Stamford Bridge, and with qualification for the Champions League still up for grabs. The caveat is, if Chelsea go on to win this season's Champions League, 4th place in the league will not qualify for next season. Harsh.

City are good. They dominate the match, but fashion few chances, though one shot is cleared off the line. There is enough to suggest that the team have not frozen on their big day, but we need that goal.

The second half progresses. The clock ticks by, though I try not to look at it. City are still struggling to fashion good chances. Then Roberto Mancini does that thing again, by making what looks like a defensive substitution when goals are needed. Nigel De Jong on, Samir Nasri off. But now, Yaya Toure can venture forward more. The clock keeps ticking. At what point do I really begin to panic, as I know City have to win this game? United are at home to Swansea City later in the day, and they will win that game.

Please score City. Please. I don't ask for much. Just do this for me, for all of us. Please.

And then.

Twenty minutes to go. There is an interchange with Sergio Aguero, and Yaya Toure, from outside the area, curls the ball majestically, low and into the corner. The net ripples. The away end erupts. Toure knee slides and there is a pile on of players. Close to me, a child is knocked over in the ensuing carnage, but he finds it all hilarious. The mood changes in an instant. It is a magnificent goal from a player who scores heavy goals and carries his brilliance with such nonchalance.

I am surely happy now? Not so, after the celebrations die down. Now I want another goal, so that there is a chance to relax, of sorts. One moment is all it takes for the league title to slip away again. Don't mess it up now. City never make it easy though, but that's probably how all football fans think about their club. Sergio Aguero misses a sitter, then misses another, after Yaya Toure trips himself up when through on goal. Newcastle miss a chance. This is torture, of the football variety.

Salvation finally arrives with two minutes of normal time remaining. The ball is passed square to Toure once more, who has ambled his way to within five yards of the goal without any Newcastle player paying him much attention. He strikes it cleanly into the back of the net. That is surely that, and the away end erupts once more.

"We're gonna win the league," is belted out by thousands. Suddenly there is a confidence that this will happen, that City are going to avenge decades of pain. The relief, joy, and adrenalin is painted large on the faces of everyone around me. I feel euphoric, there is no other word. The gut-wrenching nerves of the day, from the moment I woke up at 5am, are gone. I look at the clock, fearful of injury time still holding a surprise or two, but the home side know the game is lost. Even I don't think City can mess this up, and quietly I sing about City winning the league too.

It's a fun journey back, or at least the first half is. Soon I can drink no more, and despite the din, I fall asleep for the final 100 miles. What a day.

After the adrenalin wears off, and the buzz subsides, it dawns on me what lies ahead, as I experience a moment of clarity. The longest week of all lies ahead, and certainly the most unproductive. One more win needed, against QPR, seven days away. Until then, nothing but the wait.

The week in the office is a strange one. The idea that work will distract me is a false one. It does not, and with my concentration levels shattered, my work suffers. The office is a mix of United and City fans, with a solitary Bolton and Oldham fan thrown in for good measure. There is a general consensus to avoid all football talk, apart from one United fan who has mysteriously regained his bravado after the Derby defeat, and seems convinced City will mess it up against QPR. I do not engage, because there is little point in doing so. What will be will be. The United fan can sense the nerves. Deep down, he knows, and has admitted, that City are clear favourites for the league. But he can sense my weakness, and that of every other blue in the building. United have been there, and done it, City have not. And perhaps as crucially, QPR may need to get something from the match to avoid relegation. United travel to Sunderland, who have nothing to play for, and I have already written that off as three points for the visitors. The situation is crystal clear in my head. City need to beat QPR to win the league. The simplest of formulas.

The Final Countdown

This week is unbearable. Concentration levels are at an all-time low, and they were not particularly high beforehand. Days drag, and there is this constant knot in my stomach. I try to distract myself from what lies ahead, but any success is fleeting. Do some fans actually enjoy this?!

I want to check in on the media coverage, and I also want to avoid it, leaving me conflicted. I dip into my favoured message board, and there is a split of fans, between those who are wildly optimistic, and think Sunday will be a walk in the park, and those that are convinced City will mess it up on the big stage. There is a sub-section that try to divert talk away from the match, with chats about biscuits, the weather, TV and more. They are the sensible ones, ultimately. We're just waiting now, and there is little to be said.

What will be, will be. On Sunday me and many thousands of others will spend ninety minutes biting our nails as a collection of footballers determine our happiness for the subsequent few months.

During the week I have a vivid dream, which is more of a nightmare to be honest. In it, and I rarely remember dreams, Wayne Rooney is somehow playing for QPR, and with City winning a tense game 2-1, pops up to score a late equaliser four minutes into injury time. He celebrates his goal right in front of me. This plays on my insecurities, as during the 2009/10 season, United won three times against City with late goals. My brain remembers, clearly. I wake up, and for a few seconds experience the primal fear of not knowing whether the dream actually happened.

On the Tuesday, I am already nervous, but I console myself with the thought that it's OK, because at least the match is not that day.

On the Wednesday, I am already very nervous, but I console myself with the thought that it's OK, because at least the match is not that day.

On the Thursday, I am now extremely nervous, but I console myself with the thought that it's OK, because at least the match is not that day.

On the Friday, I am a nervous wreck, but I console myself with the thought that it's OK, because at least the match is not that day.

On the Saturday, I am almost out of excuses. I eat the unhealthiest food as a small diversion. But at least the match is not that day.

And so to Sunday, May 13th, 2012. It's weird and it's terrifying waking up knowing that the day that follows will either be one of the best or the worst of my life, with no options in between. I've spent all week trying not to think about, trying not to consider how I may feel as that final whistle blows.

May 13th, 2012

I wake up at 6am. So, this is it. The big day. A day of extreme emotion, guaranteed. Hopefully, the day I have always dreamed about. I feel dread like I have never felt before. As if I know the phone is about to ring, bringing with it terrible news. I cannot sleep, so I get up.

Again, I try to use up the empty time before I head into town. Let's hope for better results this time around.

Eventually, I walk to the newsagents, slowly, the sort of speed that used to exasperate me on a Saturday morning as my mum stopped to look in every shop window on the High Street. I create my own game of not stepping on the cracks in the pavement, then speed up to beat a fellow pedestrian to an assigned lamppost, taking the chequered flag with centimetres to spare.

I peruse the magazine section at WH Smiths. Then the books. Look at the birthday cards. All rubbish, as they have always been. Pop into the newsagents. Buy the same two packets of crisps – Salt and Vinegar Discos and Bacon Wheat Crunchies. Eat one packet on the way home, as I walk slowly once more.

Finally get back to the flat. Take off my coat, and look at the clock. Thirty-seven minutes.

For the final time this season, the routine. Bring it home, Craig. Left sock on first. Left trouser leg first. Davidoff Coolwater aftershave. Two coffees, with one sugar. Keys in right pocket. Same coat as for previous games, even if the weather hints at a thinner jacket. Walk up the street on the right side of the road, cross at the lights.

But first, I force down a bacon butty, though I have no appetite, and the food makes me gag. It is time to head to town, and there is quiet in the taxi, with the smallest of small talk occasionally punctuating the silence.

There is soon a huge crowd in the beer garden of our usual pre-match pub. The sun is out, nice day. Same routine - I cannot drink, more than a sip here and there though, the nausea overriding my natural instincts. I wanted to get drunk to take the edge off, but I cannot.

I am shaking. I feel cold on this sunny day. Have I got a fever? Just knock me out and tell me the score when I wake up. A man offers me £500 for my match ticket. I am tempted, as that is a fortune to me, but I decline. I must be there if City win.

Time moves at its own pace, and I just want the match to start. It will soon be time to get a taxi to the ground. But first, a friend suggests a photo. We ask the landlord to take it when he wanders past collecting glasses. And so there we all are, 34 of us in total, stood with forced smiles, the nerves kicking in, one last photo before our lives change forever, one way or another. What a journey it has been.

There is a good atmosphere outside the ground. My mood is not helped by the Champions scarves on sale. I hope they're not all in a bin by the end of the day. Soon I am in my seat, and there is every emotion swirling around the stadium. Everyone shakes hands as they arrive. The mood is upbeat above all else, for this is what we have all waited for.

There are backstories to the QPR match that only serve to make me more nervous. In vital games against a supposed underdog, I do not need backstories, narratives or anything similar. It's the equivalent of bad weather, the great leveller when two teams of contrasting quality take to the field. At least the forecast is fine for this match.

The first narrative concerns the QPR manager, none other than Mark Hughes, airlifted in to ensure the Hoops' survival. Hughes arrives with lingering resentment at his treatment at City, who dismissed him two and a half years ago. In between he managed Fulham for eleven months, before quitting claiming he needed new experiences. I don't wish to claim I know what he is thinking, but there must be at least a little bit of him that would love to be a party pooper on City's big day. His successor winning the league is not good for his profile. However, I am not sure how lingering resentment can make a team play better. His team need the result for their own reasons, so it should not matter.

The second narrative is the return of a City youth player who rose through the youth ranks to the first team, making over 100 appearances – Nedum Onuoha. Nedum was a talented sprinter in his youth, but thankfully decided to pursue a career in football. A talented defender, it seems Roberto Mancini didn't fancy him, the Italian bizarrely of the opinion that picking up injuries was a sign of weakness. I'm not sure what the narrative is here, as Onuoha has a love for City, so I hope both teams have a happy ending to the day.

Then there's Shaun Wright-Phillips, also now at QPR, one of my favourite ever players. This is a subplot I could do without as my mind races about the many stories that could be written on this historic day. Wright-Phillips is a true City fan, but he is professional as well, and on a day when his current team could get relegated, he is sure to give his all. It would break my heart if he contributes to City failing to win the league, but i wouldn't love him any less.

The other ex-City player representing QPR may prove even more of a problem. Joey Barton returns to the Etihad, and while once more I would not expect him to carry a hatred of the club he spent most of his best years at, he possesses the type of character that would love little more than to ruin City's day. Ultimately however, he wouldn't get near City's first team in 2012, and City will field a far superior XI that just needs to concentrate on the job, and get three points. Narratives should not be a consideration, except for nervous wrecks like me. It's down to the players now to finish the job, and immortalise themselves in the club's history.

Coping Mechanisms

I'm 6ft 1" tall. This means I can never be a world-class basketball player or top jockey. But I could be a world-class footballer. The only thing stopping me is a lack of natural talent, or the drive, application, fitness, mentality and focus needed to succeed. But on days like this, I realise with absolute clarity an overwhelming factor in why I could not succeed in any sport, at any high level. The mentality aspect touched on above.

How on earth do players deal with days like this? I have been a shambles for weeks, and I am just a spectator. We often forget that footballer are not robots, and are flawed like all of us. But success is not just about talent. A significant aspect in rising to the top is dealing with everything that surrounds the matches. The desire, the focus, and the ability not to freeze. To deliver when it matters, and to know how to prepare to succeed. Maybe it is easier to deal with the pressure when you are involved directly, as you lose the sense of hopelessness. As a player, you can make a difference.

Can footballers ever truly comprehend the weight that rests on their shoulders, greater than Atlas carrying the celestial sphere? How their actions affect the mood and well-being of millions? Their actions can be life-changing for many of us. It's not a responsibility I could handle. I have sleepless night and can be wracked with guilt for days because I declined a pay out on a flooded kitchen insurance claim.

And yet today, at least eleven players can change a club's history. This why the best players are not always those that are the most skilled. The best players know how to deal with days like this – hopefully.

The Final Game

There's electricity in the air. I still feel ill. Nauseous.

The whistle goes. This is it. Now or never.

I am writing this the day after. Already, the memory of the first half is fleeting. As expected, City dominate the ball. There are chances, but not many. No early lead to settle the nerves. Clearly that's too much to ask for.

Twenty minutes in, the inevitable news arrives. United are winning. I'm not down at the goal, as I expected it. It was always up to City to get the job done.

The half continues. There's plenty of probing, but no goal. And then, after 39 minutes, the breakthrough, from an unlikely source. Pablo Zabaleta's shot is parried by QPR keeper Paddy Kenny, and bounces into the net as he desperately scrambles back. The roof is lifted off, the release of tension palpable. Thank **** for that. A messy goal, but they all count. Deep breaths. One more goal and the title is within touching distance.

Damn, Yaya Toure was injured in the lead up to the goal, and has to go off. No need to panic, we have enough talent to cover his absence, and we've got that vital lead.

And that's how it remains at half-time. A short period to recover. I'm exhausted just watching this, experiencing it.

I don't know what to do with myself during the 15 minutes. I just want the game done, one way or the other. What to do at half-time in a football match? This seemingly short period of time can seem like little more than a moment or close to a lifetime depending on the score and prevailing weather conditions. The break never feels longer than when it is bitterly cold. Today, I am a mess. I wander, I return, I try to regulate my breathing. Come on, restart the match.

The players are back out. The tension, oh my, the tension. Just get that second goal, please. I'm praying to non-existent football gods again. They must know how we've all suffered as fans, how we deserve this day in the sun.

I could write a book on the 2nd half alone. I just wanted that 2nd goal, to enjoy a slither of relaxation, to know that all my dreams could not be shattered in a single moment. But I did not get that 2nd goal.

Just three minutes into the half, Joleon Lescott miscalculates a long ball, and Djibril Cisse slams the ball past Joe Hart to equalise for the visitors. Ninety percent of the ground is stunned into silence.

It wasn't supposed to be like this.

Seven minutes later, and I cannot believe what I am seeing. Joey Barton confirms his reputation and kicks out at Carlos Tevez. A red card follows, and as he leaves the pitch, he takes a kick at Sergio Aguero, and tries to take a few City players with him. It's bedlam, and thankfully the City players keep their cool.

Sixty-six minutes. For those that don't understand, it will sound like hyperbole, a gross overreaction, but my world implodes. Armand Traoré breaks free on the left, and his looped cross finds Jamie Mackie unmarked, who heads past Joe Hart.

I sit there in silence. Perhaps because I'm not sure I believe what has just happened, and nor do the people around me. A goal up at half-time at home to a much worse side, and soon after a man up too, and within twenty minutes everything has gone wrong. I could almost reach out and touch that Premier League title. Typical City. Why? Why? Why?!!

Why are you doing this to me? Why couldn't you just do your job one more time?

The stadium is stunned. A ripple of support breaks out, but the disbelief makes speech difficult.

There is time to turn this around. City pile forward, wave after wave of attack, but with little end result. Naturally, the opposition goalkeeper Paddy Kenny is having the game of his life. Of course he is. Of course he fucking is.

Tick, tock. Time is ebbing away. The mood in the stands is desperate.

I think about a lot in those 25 minutes, all of it bad. About taking a break from football, never going on the internet again, about how this is going to scar me, and others, for a long time to come. This may still hurt in ten years' time. I feel sorry for myself, and wonder why I can't have nice things. Why everything goes wrong. I consider my life options, and what I would do differently if I got a 2nd chance. I feel a guttural sorrow, as if I have suffered true loss. I want to start the day again. Anything to start the day again. I feel like a failure, as if this match is somehow intrinsically linked to the life choices I have made. It is symbolic of my failure to get a great job, buy a house, settle down, change the world. This football club was made for me, perhaps.

It wasn't supposed to be like this.

The clock taunts me. For once, it is moving fast. My enthusiasm ebbs away. I'm an empty shell. And with each passing minute, the hope of everyone around me drains away. They deal with this in varying ways. For most, silence. Occasional shouts of encouragement. For some, frustration. For others, pure anger, at the thought that City could mess it up when so close to glory. Typical City.

I decide that being a football supporter for 30 years hasn't been worth it. I wished that my dad had never taken me to a match. Or if he had, taken me to see a different team. If he'd taken me to see United, I would now love them, because that's how it works. I'd probably be a different person, because your football shapes you. I'd be more confident perhaps, cockier, arrogant. I don't consider those good traits, but people with them seem to do better in life.

But dad has always been a blue, so there really was no choice. This is the hand I was dealt. And right now, I've got a pair of twos, and United have just gone all in. There is another way City could be saved. If Sunderland equalised at United. But I know inherently, from the bottom of my heart, that this will not happen. United will win their game. So City must win theirs.

What am I going to do at full time? I don't want to go to the pub and sit in deathly silence with friends. I don't want to go home and sit with my own silence. I don't want anything. There's no escape from this. I don't want to feel like this. Not now, not ever again.

I know the precise moment I give up for good. When the clock hits 85 minutes. Logistically, two goals doesn't feel possible now. QPR can waste a couple of minutes here and there, and there's just not time. It's over. Their keeper makes yet another save. It's not meant to be. It's never meant to be. This is my life, a bridesmaid once more. Some people leave. I think, I don't know, I am catatonic by this stage.

And the thought that dominates above all is this: it's just not fair. None of this is fair.

Why can't I have just this one good thing happen? I don't ask for much. A takeaway on a Friday night, my health, enough money to pay the bills. And just to be happy now and then. But no, the footballing gods couldn't let me be happy. They had to ruin it all. More to the point, why get my hopes up in the first place? I wish we'd drawn with Newcastle now.

And then, we are into injury time. I think it's five minutes, it doesn't matter, unless it's twenty. There's an official with a board, but I don't glance over.

A minute of it passes. The end offers its hand. Followed by the worst summer of my life.

Another corner. David Silva swings it in, Edin Dzeko meets the cross perfectly, and the back of the net ripples.

City have equalised.

Somehow, Edin Dzeko's equaliser makes things even worse. Have you ever felt worse after your team has scored a goal? If City had lost 2-1, then yes it would feel like the world was ending. I would take a long time to get over it. But to now get an equaliser and fail by a single goal is just rubbing City's failure in my face. If City are going to mess this up, and it seems they are, at least fail in spectacular fashion, and not by the slimmest of margins.

What time was the goal? Not that it matters, but must have been just after 91 minutes. I didn't even look at the amount of injury time when the board went up, as there seemed no point. There is definitely five minutes of injury time. So there may be one chance left to save this, save my life. I'm still devoid of hope.

The end is imminent, no putting off what will follow. It will be a long evening. I bemoan my life again, in these crazy few minutes. Thirty-six years old, renting a flat where the boiler rarely works. There's mould in the bathroom. The guy upstairs has a terrible taste in trance music, which he likes to play loudly at all hours of the day. I've no money, I never have. My girlfriend dumped me because I lack ambition, and because, apparently, I am too nice, whatever that means. And now this – proof that I cannot have nice things. City are pressing, but time is almost up now. United are still winning, as everyone knew they would. Shaun-Wright-Phillips runs to the half-way line with the ball, and there is a tackle, and the ball goes out of play. It is a throw-in to them, which will kill more time, as QPR just want the draw now. Nasri is holding the ball for some reason, offering it as a sacrifice, and by the time the throw-in is taken, there is just two minutes left. I can almost feel that gut-wrenching moment. It's about to happen, no avoiding it anymore, nor its consequences.

That walk into town. Waking up tomorrow. Not fair. City at least get the ball back quickly, and drive forward. Sergio Aguero drops deep, and feeds the ball to Mario Balotelli on the edge of the area, and he falls under pressure, but manages to prod the ball forward. Aguero has continued his run forward, and..and.... it has come to him 12 yards out. A QPR defender lunges desperately, trying to block the ball. He misses. His foot connects with the foot of Aguero. Aguero stays on his feet. Aguero is through, there is 93:19 on the clock, he shoots towards goal.......

In one split-second, one singular moment in time, I am detached from the real world. This cannot be real, surely? This did not happen. How could it? I was at rock bottom, lower than I have ever been before, to a place closer to hell than five relegations could ever take me. All around me, there is something happening that I know instantly is never to be repeated, never matched, never beaten. In basic terms, pure, unadulterated carnage. Bedlam – there's another word, and joy like I have never experienced before, and perhaps never will again. I am hugging three friends at the same time. I am hugging strangers. I am moving in random directions, I am in the row behind, I am in the aisle. I am bouncing off seats, and it hurts, and I could not care less. The hurt is over. A guttural sound that is unique to this moment in time resonates around the entire ground. I notice the faces of those beside me, wide-eyed, pure happiness, the faces of those who, and this is no exaggeration, have seen their lives transformed with one swing of a boot. Wild screams, arms raised to the heavens, uncontrollable, unrehearsed, unbelievable. None of us know how to act so we revert to primitive beings. A friend appears from nowhere, one who was sat ten rows away and he jumps on my back. I don't know where I am anymore. Songs spring into life, but it is mostly still screaming. I take my first glance towards the pitch since I last looked to check the linesman did not have his flag raised. The scenes on the pitch are similar to those in the stands. I will relive this moment a thousand times, but it cannot match what I feel right now. Bottle it up, and drink it in. I wish I could. I've fallen in love all over again.

Right now, in this moment in time, this – THIS - is how it feels to be City.

No, this is how it can feel to be a football fan.

What is this feeling? I can't describe it. OK, I'll try. It's overwhelming, from another world. I was broken, then in an instant, was fixed. How do you deal with that, how do you react? How do you process what happened? Perhaps I never will.

Pure, unfiltered joy. I could cry, but I don't. Others are though. It is chaos - beautiful, raw, chaos. I hug and I hug, I scream and I punch the air a million times. This is it. This is everything. I am kicked, shoved, kissed, my hair is grabbed, and I am no longer in my seat, nowhere near it to be honest.

The air is sucked out of the stadium, and the noise. The noise. I've never heard anything like it before.

I suddenly feel dizzy. I stop jumping around, and stay still. Catch my breath. A sudden shiver pulses down my spine. I look around me. The wonder of it all. A level of happiness, in the moment, that can never be repeated, never replicated, never matched. The pinnacle of my football-supporting life.

But in this moment, I realise how lucky I am to experience it once. Not every football fan will.

It's the unexpected nature of it all. From the depths to the heights in a single second. There is nothing else in life that can come close. Life's happiest events are usually expected, they don't taunt you before giving you a huge slap in the face. You see them coming, get to prepare, and this helps you deal with them.

I realise I am exhausted. Bruised, too. I am hugging complete strangers. It's like we've been friends forever. Everyone living in the moment.

The entire stadium is delirious. QPR have stayed up, so it's time for them to celebrate too.

Oh shit, the match hasn't actually finished. The stress returns in an unstoppable wave that almost knocks me off my feet. And gently drifts away as soon as the game restarts, when it becomes abundantly clear that QPR have no intention of seeking an equaliser.

Twenty seconds before Sergio Aguero changed my life forever, the news filtered through to the QPR fans that they were staying up, whatever the result at the Etihad. The QPR bench quickly realised too, and by the time the game restarted, the players knew the score, literally and metaphorically. This was going to be a day of celebration for every fan in the ground. And for quite a few now desperately trying to get back in having previously given up hope.

We stay in the ground for a long time. There is a pitch invasion as the full-time whistle blows, of course. It takes a long time for it to clear, and no one cares. The players are back out, the trophy is lifted, and it is all a blur, so that is all you are getting from me. It was beautiful, I know that.

As we leave the ground, and walk towards the main road, my friends hesitate to hug a man they know. I've never seen such joy on so many faces.

I hang back and take a moment. Look around me.

This. This, is everything. Be it a title win, a promotion, a last-minute winner, a Derby victory, or just a big win. This is what it is all about. This is the payback for the moods, the defeats, the stress, the pressure, anxiety, arguments, disagreements, false hope, let downs, dejection, the damage done to relationships.

How wonderful it is to be a football fan. What better life could there be?

I am getting so many messages on my phone I cannot catch up. A United fan kindly says well done, and that City deserved it. Amongst the other messages, I see one from Claire:

Well done! X

I smile, but don't reply.

I'd be lying if I gave you a blow-by-blow account of the night that followed. Drinking, chanting, a heaving mass of bodies, my voice lost. Banners were pinned up in the pub, and the singing was relentless. A lot of beer was drunk, and a lot spilt. I remember my friend and his father hugging in the corner of the pub for minutes on end, tears in their eyesI fell over in the toilet. My phone battery was empty by 9pm. I ended the night on Jack Daniels & Coke, with a lock-in. Exhausted and delirious at the same time. What had happened? Was it real?

I sleep well that night.

I bruise easily, and I wake up to discover a large purple mark stretching down my right thigh. My personal memento of the previous day, and all that entailed. I look at it with pride.

It's obvious to say that Aguero's goal was the defining moment of my football supporting life. I don't think it is. It was the 25 minutes between QPR going ahead and City winning the league. That defined me more than anything else that has ever gone before. That period made me question everything, and afterwards, once I realised everything was going to be OK after all, changed the way I looked at things. Changed my relationship with my football team, hopefully for the better. Freed me of my "woe is me" attitude, at least for a short while. My team will hurt me again, many times, in the future. They will make me disappointed, frustrated, angry, and down. But after this, how can I not forgive them? How can I not be thankful? Having said all that, memories can be short. No doubt I'll be back to my old self the moment something goes against City next season.

Premier League dreams have come true in blue. Drink it in.

That period created the unique noise that followed. A noise I will never hear again, a noise I cannot do justice to with words. A sound like no other. What is it? It's oohs and aahs and shrieks and whatever noise comes out of mouths at a time of extreme emotion. It cannot be replicated because it cannot be manufactured.

This game shows how the legacy of a player or manager often relies on very fine lines. History is written by the winners, and this feels like proof. Roberto Mancini is assured legendary status, whatever happens from now on. But what if Sergio Aguero has sliced his shot wide? Mancini would probably be considered a failure, a bottler. His fiery nature and maverick ways would be ripped apart in fine detail, and his fall-out with Carlos Tevez declared the moment City lost the title. Everything would be portrayed in a different light, due to one kick of a football.

In not saying that would be right, as the performance is on the players, there is only so much the manager can do. But history may not have judged him so kindly.

So if I could replay that day again, would I want it any other way? A comfortable 4-0 win would have provided the same result, but far fewer stories - it would have meant we missed out on the greatest Premier League moment of them all. And my greatest moment too, never to be surpassed.

I wish my dad was there to see it all. To experience it with me. But that is the way of life, and near death. After we all go, there will be many wonderful experiences and memories formed that others will live through, but not us. A shame that dad might be missing out on a golden era, but we had that FA Cup triumph, and a lot more besides.

I will be happy if I live my life with a par score. I'm privileged and fortunate to be born when I was and where I was. If I have an OK life within that context, then I have lived an easier life than most. How ridiculous it must seem to many to factor in the result of a football match into the equation, but that is what I will now do. Every rejection, every false turn, every down moment, has been wiped by the rustle of a net. I'm now under par. Consider hitting three successive hole-in-ones and you will get a rough idea of what this means to me, and others.

Time To Walk Away

I have set myself a new life goal. Not along the traditional lines of wife, two kids, house in the burbs and a dog named Bouncer, though I am not opposed to such things. No, despite what it has given me this week, which was everything, my goal is to work out how to find true happiness, and to ensure that it never rides on the result of a football match. For it is something that I need to make happen myself.

Deep down, I know that I will never get close to accomplishing that life goal, but it's a nice thought. That title run-in was too stressful to repeat - but I have spent my whole life fighting this dependency on football, and it has been a losing battle.

The Aftermath

I consume the internet for at least two days. Work can wait. I watch a replay of THAT goal a hundred times over the following week, and even though I know Aguero scores, I get palpitations every single time. What if he had missed? What if he had gone down, and a league title rested on a penalty? That would have been too much. How can I be so nervous about something I know the outcome of?!

I don't know what the future holds, and I don't want to know. I know one thing, that the QPR match, or the end of it, is and always will be the pinnacle of my football-supporting life. There is no situation that could top it, no script the greatest writers could create. Everything after this may be an anti-climax, but that's OK. Because I'm lucky to have experienced this moment, so I cannot complain about anything that follows. I will complain, repeatedly, but I shouldn't. Hopefully there's plenty more joy to be had, more trophies, trips to Wembley, European jaunts and some amazing players in sky blue.

Twitter is tremendous fun for many weeks. A tweet of mine goes semi-viral, and Joleon Lescott likes it. This free website allows me to connect with hundreds of fans I would not otherwise have known existed. Such a collective joy, and the stories that emerge about the day will live with me, all of us, forever. Social media does have its uses after all.

There's a parade in town. The city centre is a sea of blue, and the weather's OK too. The police estimate a crowd of 100,000 and it is an amazing and quite surreal feeling to see the city centre taken over by a single fanbase - United fans are understandably giving the area a wide berth. Earlier in the day, I thought the idea of standing on a street corner to watch a bus full of players trundle pass was not the most appetising prospect. I was wrong, it feels great. I get some good photos, and when I look back at them, I am sure in one Vincent Kompany is holding aloft the Premier League trophy solely for me.

A man can dream.

I get back home in the early evening, sober yet intoxicated. On the way home, I pick up one more chippy tea. With a scallop on the side, plenty of vinegar. Actually, they're not that bad.

Football, and the friends I have made along the way, has taken me to Hamburg, Cologne, Liverpool and Rome. To a Middlesborough Wetherspoons at 10am, into many a drunken taxi ride home. I've woken up in the bath of a stranger's hotel room in Birmingham. I've temporarily fallen out with a friend due to a drunken argument over the merits of Mario Balotelli. I've maxed out a credit card to watch my team, had punches thrown at me because of the shirt I was wearing, cried with joy as I walked down Wembley Way because I felt my club had a future after a play-off miracle. I've felt at my lowest and at my highest because of football. I've sung with strangers in foreign lands, and drunk endless cheap shots in a Danish bar with a hairy and scary man called Erik. I've slept in train stations, missed flights, and spent a fortune. I've sat glued to a radio as I listened to my team being relegated. I've rushed to Maine Road with a flag and an inflatable banana to celebrate my team getting promoted. I've jibbed into at least two grounds having failed to get a ticket. Been locked in a coach toilet on the way to Highbury. Fainted after an important goal. I've kissed the badge after winning a game of three-and-in. I've used jumpers and rocks and coats and sticks and cones as goalposts. I've had letters slating my team published in the Manchester Evening News. I've skipped round my living room after a late goal brought home my accumulator. I've bet on my team to lose, but rarely on them to win. I've made lifelong friends and a couple of enemies. Drunk far too much but never regretted it. Been sick in a taxi, Wembley toilets, and a Premier Inn near Brighton. I've fallen asleep in a ground. Got a very small tattoo on my backside (he remembered). I've lost my inhibitions like never before. I've felt part of something important.

I've felt like I belong.

44 Years

"I was me, but now he's gone." – Metallica.

I rearrange his bedding, as he asks me if I have had my ice cream. He is back to my childhood. There would often be ice pops and cheap orange lollies in the freezer during the summer months, but I associate ice cream with the van that would circle the neighbourhood for half the year, and with the seaside. I would bite off the bottom of the cone and suck the ice cream out through the hole.

I've brought two Magnums along as it's a warm day, though my dad is not quick enough to prevent much of it covering his hand. We're talking food again, as dad always likes to talk about meal times of old. He says he used to go to the chip shop every Saturday lunchtime, not just on matchdays, and he always had the same thing. Sausage, chips and gravy. I remember this. Have I mentioned this already? I was weird and had chips with sweet and sour sauce. When I was finished and had taken all the plates into the kitchen, I was allowed an hour of Grandstand on the BBC.

These thoughts are me regressing once more. My dad is looking back, that is natural. Now I get to look forward at last. Many would argue that supporting a football team is character-building. Perhaps that is true, it's just that it may not build the character you desired. My football team has been good for my character recently though, so there is hope.

We're all trying to recapture our youth, or the joy of it, of childhood, and its innocence. As a child you don't realise you're living your best life, how could you? Now I'm beaten and worn down by the world, and all I want is one day of playing French cricket in the cul-de-sac near my house and cycling no-handed around Heaton Park.

But Sunday made me feel alive again. Even as a child, I could not have experienced joy like that at the moment Sergio Aguero twirled his shirt above his head.

I help my dad take a sip of water. He is looking very old now. There is a period of silence. Then his face changes, as if he has had just had a Eureka moment.

"Did they do it, son? Did City do it?"

I pause. Dad has spilt some drink on his bedside drawer, and I get a piece of kitchen roll and dab up the mess. He's not called me son for many years.

"Did they do it, son? Did City do it?"

I sit on the bed, and put an arm around my dad.

"They did it dad. They did it."

"But when I tell you how they did it, I don't think you'll believe me."

Howard Hockin is a writer and podcaster, most notably for the Manchester City podcasts 93:20 and Blue Moon.

He has written many books about Manchester City, all season reviews, and a couple about other things from his distant past.

You can find him on Twitter at @howiehok3434.

Oh, and his favourite ever player is Sergio Aguero.

Printed in Great Britain
by Amazon